# SURRENDERING TO THE RAKE

~ & ~

# AN INDECENT WAGER

GEORGETTE BROWN

Published by Wind Color Press
Copyright © 2017

# SURRENDERING TO THE RAKE

# CHAPTER ONE

Though the clouds shrouded the night in blackness, obscuring all but shadows from view, the lone woman standing at the gates pulled her veil more securely about her face with restless, trembling hands. Every little noise—the stirring of the leaves in the trees, the scurry of some small animal, the crunch of pebbles at her feet—made her jump. At any moment she expected her cousin to descend upon her with eyes ablaze, denouncing her treachery and forswearing the sisterhood they had shared these past years.

Heloise Merrill cringed and glanced down the path, both dreading and desperate for the arrival of the carriage. Her cousin Josephine would not understand that, were it not for the affection the two of them shared, Heloise would not be standing on an open road by herself in the middle of the night, pretending to be her cousin.

She tugged at her veil.

Would the footmen recognize that she was not Josephine Merrill? Her form alone could betray her.

Josephine possessed a slender body with delicate, sloping shoulders whereas Heloise had square shoulders and flesh to spare about her arms and waist. The veil hid her countenance—her round face, full cheeks and rosebud mouth. Josephine had a physiognomy that tapered at the chin, wide lips, a pert nose and slender arched brows.

The glow of a lantern approached. Heloise willed her feet to stay and not carry her back to the safety of the home she shared with her cousin and uncle, Jonathan Merrill, who had kindly taken Heloise in years ago when her parents had both succumbed to consumption. Alas, her uncle would not be home for a sennight, leaving Heloise the elder of the household. She had been tempted to send for him immediately when she had discovered the note intended for Josephine—an invitation to three shameless nights of profligacy with Sebastian Cadwell, the Earl of Blythe—but even then her uncle would not have been able to return in time. Josephine might never forgive her, but she could not allow her cousin to throw away a life of promise on a youthful fancy for a dangerous man—one of the worst rakes in England.

"Miss Merrill?" the driver inquired after alighting from his perch.

After forcing herself to exhale, Heloise nodded. Accepting his assistance with averted eyes, as if the driver might see through her veil, she stepped into the carriage. A whip cracked the air, and the carriage lurched forward. It would be hours before she arrived at her destination, the Château Follet, so named for its owner, a French expatriate.

Some dubbed it the Château of Debauchery.

How many victims had the earl claimed? Heloise wondered, unable to settle herself comfortably in the rich upholstery of the carriage seats. Neither the driver nor the footman had sneered at her or indicated in any way that they thought her a wanton woman. They did not even ask why she traveled sans a portmanteau or valise. Was it because they were accustomed to picking up women in the middle of the night for their master? Heloise shuddered to think how closely Josephine had come to ruining herself—and that prospect remained lest Heloise returned successful. She simply had to succeed. Her attempts to reason with Josephine had failed.

*"What has the Earl of Blythe to recommend himself but a rugged countenance?"* Heloise had asked.

*"You would not understand, Heloise,"* Josephine had returned.

*"What would I not understand?"* she had pressed.

Tossing her luxuriant flaxen curls, Josephine had replied, *"The ways of a man and a woman."*

*"I am six years your senior. You are but a babe at nine and ten. I have glimpsed more of human nature than you, Josephine."*

*"My dear Heloise, you may have more years than I, and I mean no cruelty, but your experience with men is decidedly limited."*

Heloise had not revealed to Josephine that her experience with the opposite sex was not as lacking as Josephine would believe. Granted, Josephine had no shortage of suitors whereas Heloise had entertained but one in recent years. But the dearth of suitors had not diminished her ability to observe humankind, and she knew a rogue when she saw one. People had a tendency to overlook the shortcomings in a man such as Sebastian Cadwell because of his title, wealth and breeding.

When it had become clear that her disapproval of Josephine's choice of company was having the unintended consequence of making her cousin even more attached to Sebastian, Heloise had attempted to reason with the earl himself. She had requested an audience with him on numerous occasions, but he had refused all of her attempts to engage him in conversation until she had managed one evening to accost him as he emerged from his box at the theater.

\* \* \* \* \*

"I would have a word with you, your lordship," Heloise had said hastily before he could turn to ignore her.

He had stared down at her with brown eyes so dark they appeared black. With dark hair waving over a wide brow, the firm, square jaw of a man who knows what he wants and a subtle cleft of the chin to denote a masculinity matured, the earl was more imposing than she remembered. His stylish hat sat at smart attention upon his head. His double-breasted coat with matching high collar fit him snugly, emphasizing his broad shoulders and tall frame. Lord Blythe had always been considered a swell of the first stare.

"You have not responded to my written requests to speak with you," she added, trying not to be intimidated by his height. He seemed to command

Made in the USA
San Bernardino, CA
08 February 2020

64210826R00100

more space than his body actually occupied. "I think it rather discourteous of you not to have granted me an audience."

He smiled—an unnerving curl of the lips. Sensuous lips. Heloise snapped her attention to the matter at hand. Gracious, why was she staring at the man's lips?

"You would find me more discourteous, I assure you, had I accepted your request, Miss Merrill."

At her surprised pause, he continued, "I know what it is you intend to speak to me of, and I had thought to spare us both from the conclusion you would draw of me upon hearing my response."

His words took her breath away.

"Ah, I was right," he noted. "I can tell at this moment you think me audacious and arrogant."

She flushed, perturbed that he should have correctly guessed her thoughts.

"Let us now part ways," he suggested, "before I offend you further."

Heloise attempted to grab at words, to form some manner of coherent retort, but failed. Worse still, she had not realized her mouth hung open until he curled his forefinger gently beneath her chin and closed her lips. Horrified, she was only too glad when he tipped his hat and took his leave. Her heart was pounding madly—she wished from anger alone but had to admit it was his touch that had unsettled her more. A warm wave had rushed over her body, and she understood for the first time how Josephine could be captivated by this man. A man she had hitherto disdained. And now considered more dangerous than ever.

\* \* \* \* \*

There would be no mouth dumbly agape this time, Heloise promised herself as the Château Follet loomed before her. She intended to provide Sebastian Cadwell the set-down he deserved. This time she was prepared to do battle and emerge the victor. If she did not, she would have risked her cousin's affection for naught. For hours after discovering the letter from the earl, Heloise had struggled with the idea of reasoning with Josephine again. Surely Josephine knew that the earl would merely use her for the pleasures of the flesh, then cast her aside as he had done with so many women before her? But the numerous suitors that Josephine had entertained must have engendered many a romantic notion in her young head.

Or worse, perhaps Josephine would not care.

This was the only way, Heloise affirmed to herself as she alighted from the carriage. Waiting at the steps of the château, an abigail named Annabelle greeted her quietly and gently.

"I will show you to your room, madam," Annabelle said.

Heloise considered scurrying back into the carriage. Perhaps there was another means to accomplish her goal, one that she had overlooked, one that did not require her to be here? But when she turned to seek the carriage, it had disappeared around the corner.

*What a ninny you are, Heloise Merrill*, she chided herself. She had heard scandalous things occurred at the home of Madame Follet, a French widow rumored to have known the notorious Marquis de Sade in her previous life.

The abigail showed Heloise upstairs to a room with a magnificent bed with cornices atop its posts and a pleated valance, a veneered writing desk, a sofa and chairs upholstered in silk, a mahogany chest of drawers and a vanity with inlaid top. The many golden candelabras and the floral silk wallpaper adorning the walls lent a comforting warmth to the room.

"His lordship requested this room for you," Annabelle explained. "It be our finest. We call it the Empress Room."

"Is…is His lordship here?" Heloise inquired, trying to remain calm.

"He arrives soon, I believe, but he has arranged for your wardrobe. Shall I assist you now into your nightdress?"

"That won't be necessary," Heloise responded, stepping away before the woman could touch her.

Annabelle look puzzled.

"I shall ring if I find I need your assistance, shall I?"

Annabelle frowned, perhaps wondering if Heloise would summon her from her bed at an inconvenient time.

"You are welcome to retire for the evening," Heloise assured her. She had no intention of staying for long. Once she was done with the earl, she would request a post-chaise to take her home. Taking a seat on the bed, she waited for Sebastian Cadwell.

\* \* \* \* \*

Sebastian handed his hat and gloves to one of Madame Follet's footmen and considered heading up to the room where Josephine Merrill would be waiting. He paused, lacking desire. Indeed, he had had little inclination to invite her here, but the minx had worn down his resistance. Her determination had pleased his vanity. It had been years since he had allowed himself to be embroiled in a relationship with one as young as Miss Josephine, but her youthfulness belied her familiarity with men. He knew she had lifted her skirts beneath at least two friends of his.

Not looking in upon her would be impolite. Perhaps she would still be asleep. Would he attempt to wake her with a kiss or would he be relieved and head to his own room for a moment of solitude?

*What the bloody hell is the matter with me?* He had never hesitated before, had never known his eros to waver. He enjoyed all manner of women. Why not the lovely and charming Josephine Merrill? His friends, if they knew his thoughts, would question his manhood or suggest that old age was settling in upon him though he had turned but two and thirty earlier this year.

"Cadwell, *mon cheri*!" Marguerite Follet greeted him.

The lady of the house, in stylish *dishabille* and a golden turban, looked radiant, as much a beauty at forty as she had been at twenty.

Sebastian kissed her extended hand.

"My maid tells me your lady friend arrived," she notified him. "She is not what I would have ascribed to your tastes. She seems almost *virginal*. I thought you never did virgins."

"I don't," he responded resolutely.

"Ah, then there is more than meets the eye with

your mademoiselle. I think, at the least, you need have no worry from Lord Devon."

Sebastian thought her comment strange, for Lord Devon had been known to try his luck with all the maidens at Lady Follet's.

"I warn you he arrived yesterday and has with him *two* lady-birds. *Twin sisters*," Lady Follet continued. "And Anne Wesley is here as well. I do wish Lord Harsdale would stop inviting her. I dread unhappy people, and she is as acrimonious as they come. You would not believe what she said to me—that you were a lover of *middling* abilities."

He started. That had never been said of him before.

"Of course she speaks from a bitter heart. Everyone knows how long she pined for you."

Had Anne counterfeited the ecstatic cries—cries so loud he had thought he might never hear properly again—when she had been with him? Sebastian wondered. It was hard to believe. He had never questioned his intuition when it came to the art of lovemaking. Nonetheless, he felt a stir in his groin.

"Goodness knows there are few to equal you where *that* is concerned," Lady Follet added with a telling flush in her cheeks. "When you are done with your mademoiselle and have a wish to renew your acquaintance with *me*…"

Sebastian bowed, recalling with fondness the moments of passion they had shared on occasion. "You honor me, my lady."

A sigh escaped her lips. "I would that it be soon, Cadwell. I fear one day you will have no use for me and my château."

"That could never be."

Her golden-brown eyes surveyed him with a depth he had never felt before. "I wonder, Cadwell, that you might not someday take a mistress or more permanent lover? Even a wife?"

"My record speaks for itself. Any woman who accepts my invitation understands that the three nights here represent the end, not the beginning, of an affair."

"And have you never requested to see a woman again when you have done with her here?"

"Never. What better way to conclude a liaison than with three nights of unforgettable passion? Why wait until I tire of her or she of me? Why tempt what would no doubt be an awkward or painful end?"

"What a pragmatist you are, Cadwell."

He inclined his head in acknowledgement.

"Love knows no pragmatism."

"My dear," Sebastian said, eying her with care, "have you partaken of tainted waters?"

Lady Follet pursed her lips. "It is only…well, your lady…never mind. I will not keep you."

With a gracious bow and kiss to her hand, he took his leave and headed up the stairs to see Miss Josephine. He resolved that he would make it worth her while. He certainly would not have her echoing Anne Wesley's sentiments, fabricated or otherwise. The halls would ring with the cries of joy he would wrest from his lovely guest. And then he would bid Miss Josephine *adieu*, as he had to the dozens of others who had preceded her, and send he on her way to a better future.

As he headed down the hall, he felt a renewed sense of spirit. The desire he had lacked moments ago returned with new vigor. He would take Miss

Josephine, awake or not, into his arms and have her swooning like never before.

* * * * *

Heloise clasped and unclasped her hands several times as she stood looking out the window at the descending moon. To her surprise, she had fallen asleep for an hour or two on the luxurious feather mattress. She was hungry and considering ringing the maid for something to eat when she heard footsteps approaching. It was *him*. Somehow she knew it was him. The long strides, the swift and confident tread could belong to none other than the Earl of Blythe.

A knock, and then the door opened. Heloise continued to stare out the window, telling herself that she would not be intimidated by this man.

"Good evening, my dear…"

Letting out a breath, Heloise turned to face him. He stood on the threshold, his form filling much of the doorframe. His tailored cutaway coat with brass buttons, fitted buff pantaloons, perfectly tied cravat and gleaming Hessians made her aware of how mussed her own appearance must be, her gown rumpled from having fallen asleep on the bed and her hair flying in wisps about her face. His eyes narrowed at her. Feeling herself falter beneath his imposing gaze, she lifted her chin.

"Where is Miss Josephine?" he asked.

The coldness in his tone sent a shiver down her spine. Bracing herself, she replied, "Safe from harm. Safe from you."

"Harm? What harm did you imagine she would

come to?"

That he should ask that question amazed and riled her. Did he think her a simpleton?

"Surely you could not be so dull of wit, your lordship?" she returned, pleased that she managed a rejoinder. "You may be devoid of morals but I thought at least you did not lack in perception."

Little flames lit his eyes.

"You would take her innocence and ruin her," Heloise accused.

"Innocence?" he echoed. "Miss Merrill, how well do you know your cousin?"

She took a sharp breath. The man was insufferable.

"Better than you," Heloise said. "She is far too respectable a person to merit your attentions."

Is that a smirk floating on his lips? she wondered.

"She is indeed," he allowed, "and as such will not suffer the injury you fear."

"It is quite well known what manner of depravity occurs here, sir!"

"No one save Lady Follet would have known she was here—lest you spoke of it."

Heloise felt her cheeks burning at the suggestion that she would have exposed her cousin.

"I spoke of this to no one when I intercepted your note to her," she said. "And how could you protect her identity here? You will forgive me if I do not profess great confidence in the likes of Lady Follet!"

"Miss Merrill, you are free to believe what you will. As for Lady Follet, you speak too hastily of a lady you know not," he said with an edge to his voice.

Heloise felt a stab of remorse for speaking harshly, but she had no need for the likes of *him* to point that out to her.

"I assumed…" she attempted, noticing with worry that the pupils of his eyes constricted.

"Why are you here, Miss Merrill?"

"You would not grant me an audience. And I would have you listen to me. I would have you listen!"

The earl folded his arms and waited. His frown did not diminish.

"If there is a shred of decency in you," she began.

He lifted his brows. "I thought I was devoid of morals."

She winced, regretting her earlier words, but there was nothing to be done. She could not retract what she had said, so she forged ahead.

"You have no need of someone like Josephine. Someone of your, well, stature can command any number of other women. Josephine is not worth your time."

"Rather harsh words for a cousin you adore."

"I meant—" she bristled.

"I know what you meant, Miss Merrill, but my mind has not changed on the matter since last we met, and I do not appreciate attempts to meddle in my affairs. I wonder that your cousin approves of it, but I take it she does not realize you are here?"

Again, she flushed. "I am here on her behalf, even if she would not approve of what I do. I realize I risk her affection, but I could not stand idly by and watch her demise. She may not know it, but she requires my aid."

"Noble if not condescending sentiments. Your cousin is a grown woman, not in leading strings."

"She is young and does not appreciate the arts a man of your sort would employ."

This time it was he who turned color. "A man of my sort?"

Would he have her explain all to him? Heloise wondered, sensing a dangerous pit opening up before her.

"I think you know to what I allude," she evaded.

"If by that you mean your shallow view of my association with women…"

Heloise blinked. *He* was the rake and would yet criticize *her* character? The man was beyond monstrous.

He continued, "I quite understand people of *your* sort and how threatened you feel by my enlightened position on the fairer sex."

"Enlightened? Is that how you defend your wanton ways?"

He clucked his tongue. "Tsk, tsk. You make it sound vulgar, Miss Merrill. Why scorn the innate urges, the natural passions of our bodies?"

Her heart began to pound once more. Something in the way he spoke, the rich tenor of his voice, the enunciation—as if he were caressing the words—made her skin warm.

"The rhetoric of one who lacks the resolve to resist the base desires…" she began, but her tone lacked confidence even to her own ears.

He took a step toward her, and despite the lethargy she had felt from her journey and lack of sleep, every nerve in her body came to life.

"Are you possessed of such resolve, Miss Merrill?" he inquired.

His gaze seemed to probe into her past, and she was sure he saw it all.

"That is none of your concern and irrelevant to the matter at hand," she said quickly.

"You made it my concern when you chose to meddle in my affairs," he replied grimly, advancing another step.

"I think I am not possessed of the same, er, passions as you," she answered, taking a step back.

"Indeed? How sad. Perhaps that can be changed."

"I have no wish to change."

"You may feel differently in three days' time."

Three days' time? What did he mean by that? Instinctively, she glanced toward the door, her escape, but it was too far. And *he* stood in her path.

"I have no plans to keep my own company for the next three days," he elaborated. "And as you have deprived me of Miss Josephine, you will have to take her place."

"I have no intention of staying," she protested, trying to stave off the panic that gripped her heart. But it was not the fear of immediate harm that alarmed her. It was…the flush of excitement coursing in her body, a sensation reminiscent of a time long ago when she did not ignore her curiosity or the urges of the flesh.

"Your intentions matter not. My coach will return you home only on my command."

"You mean to keep me here? Against my will?" she cried.

"You came of your own free will, Miss Merrill. I would have advised against it."

"I am to be your prisoner?" She attempted with

what little indignation she could muster to mask her agitation.

He advanced toward her, but she stepped back until the back of her knees struck the bed. The nearness of his body took the air from her. The flush in her body grew.

"Do you know what I do with meddlers?" he asked.

Trapped between him and the bed behind her, all she could do was hold his gaze. Her mind grasped for a rejoinder but came up empty.

"I discipline them, Miss Merrill."

# CHAPTER TWO

He saw fear in those bright almond-shaped eyes of hers.

*Good*, Sebastian thought. The little meddler needed a lesson.

Blocked from escape, she reminded him of a mouse trapped in a corner. He advanced a final step toward her, taking away the last shred of space between them, daring her to speak. Her silence gratified him. He waited to see if she would push him away or slap him in the face—he had received his fair share of those from women desperate to hold on to a semblance of propriety when inwardly they yearned to be seduced—but such an action would require her to touch him, and Miss Merrill leaned away from him so that her bosom would not graze his chest.

"You…" She faltered.

With one motion, he grasped her by the wrist, brought her arm behind her, and pushed her over his knees as he sat upon the bed.

Miss Merrill inhaled sharply but did not struggle. She lay still on top of him.

Sebastian observed the curve of her rump through her muslin and felt a sudden tug at his crotch. His hand itched to palm her arse, but he had meant only to scare her, not punish her.

"We could start with a good spanking," he said.

Was that a whimper he heard? As she was lying facedown, he could not see her expression. She made no movement. Curious, he placed his hand on the arch of one buttock. This time she flinched but remained where she was, even though he had loosened his hold on her wrist enough that she could have wrested herself away from him.

*She wants to be spanked*, he realized. A low, burning desire pulsed in his groin. Despite his earlier suggestion that she take the place of her cousin, he was all too cognizant that Miss Heloise Merrill was not Miss Josephine. Nonetheless, he was not a man to deprive a woman.

Raising his hand above her, he brought it down on the buttock he had caressed seconds before—tame but sharp enough to command attention. Again she flinched but said nothing. There was more to this Miss Merrill than he had first perceived. To his further surprise, he felt a maddening rush of desire crashing into him. Desire he had lacked earlier. He suddenly wanted to show Miss Merrill all the joys of Château Follet. Wanted to take her senses to a realm she had never known before.

He tempered his desire. This was Heloise Merrill. Not some bit of muslin. He slapped her other cheek through her gown. Her arse had such a lovely, substantive curve to it. Some women appeared to have no arse at all. He wanted to see Miss Merrill bare.

Wanted to feel her plumpness. He decided he would and massaged one buttock. *Superb.* He would enjoy giving her a sound spanking.

*No.* He intended to give her a set-down—not to engage in anything more.

As if coming to her senses, Miss Merrill tried to push herself up. He promptly pushed her back down. Now came her indignation, the blush of anger, but she would see that she was no match for him.

"I'm not finished with you yet," he told her. "Lie still."

She either did not perceive or chose not to listen to his directive for she continued to struggle. The grinding of her pelvis against his thigh caused the blood to course boldly through his groin.

"Lie still," he commanded again and emphasized his words with a harsher slap to her derrière. God, how he wanted to hear the sound of her arse sans the gown and petticoats, but he had to proceed with patience with this one. He wanted to frighten her a little—that was part of the arousal—but he also wanted her to trust him.

"I am loath to issue my demands twice, Miss Merrill," he informed her. "Now take your punishment like a good girl."

He could guess her internal dialogue. She *was* a good girl. That was perhaps the problem. Perhaps she had never been punished and was bored with being the good girl. Perhaps she had been punished too often before she became the good girl and wanted a return to the days when she wasn't so good.

She lay still across his thigh as he delivered several sharp blows. Was it his imagination or had she lifted her arse higher to greet his hand? He smacked her several more times before pausing to note her quickened breath, the stillness of her body and the flush upon her skin. His own body felt warm and he wished he had removed his coat earlier. His desire was hard with the weight of her upon him.

"How did that please you, Miss Merrill?" he asked, his breath less steady than he would have liked.

"Please me?" she returned, incredulous.

"Do not be so surprised by it, Miss Merrill."

As if to prove his implication, he reached toward her ankle and slid his hand under the hem of her gown. She gasped when his hand came in contact with her stocking-clad leg. Her body jumped at the touch, but she could do far worse if she truly loathed what was happening. Gently he drifted his hand up the silk until he reached the softness of her bare thigh—a hundred times smoother and more delectable than the feel of silk. Heady with anticipation, he reached under her arse, between her thighs, and when he connected with her wetness, he closed his eyes, his breath ragged.

The blood was pounding in his groin, and he allowed a husky quality to creep into his voice. "Your body, Miss Merrill, proves the possibilities."

Running his hand around her thigh, he palmed a buttock. *Glorious.* He grasped the flesh more firmly and heard her groan. Flipping the dress and petticoats over her waist, he laid bare the prize. Two perfectly rounded orbs, as unblemished as those of a babe, gleamed in the dim light of the candles. He licked his bottom lip as if he were about to feed on a succulent cut of beefsteak. He delivered a sharp slap with the back of his hand and watched in delight as the mound of flesh quivered.

"How many, Miss Merrill?"

"Hmmm?" came the dazed voice from beneath the layers of fabric.

He gave her a formidable swat.

"Four," she answered quickly.

Sebastian smiled to himself. She could be trained.

"Eight it is," he said. "If I have to repeat myself again, we will triple the number."

Greedily, his hand slapped at her arse. The smack of bare flesh to bare flesh rang in his ears as melodious as a symphony. When he was done, he gazed with satisfaction at the red imprints his hand had left upon her pale skin. He could smell her arousal and confirmed it when he slid his hand between her and found her wetter than before. His erection pressed painfully against her hip.

Abruptly, he stood and pulled her to one of the bedposts.

"What are you—" she protested when he pulled her wrists around the post and tied them with a cord he had yanked from the bed curtains.

Stepping back, he admired her form pressed against the bedpost. Miss Merrill was not unattractive. Her rounded figure reminded him of Ruben's portrait of Hélène Fourment. Supple. Ripe. He could see himself entwining his fingers in her lustrous dark hair. She had a complexion free of blemish and that required little in the way of powder or rouge. And those voluptuous lips...

A sense of remorse crept into him as he observed how Miss Merrill's bottom lips quivered. She had very full lips. More succulent than her cousin's. He wondered how such lips would feel beneath his own. He imagined taking her mouth would be like sinking into a rich, sweet strawberry.

His head swam with lust, and he needed to clear it before he did something he did not intend—such as tearing the clothes from her and ravishing her. He reminded himself of the anger that he had felt earlier. The impudence of this woman, to foil his plans for a pleasant weekend and deprive him of the joys of exploring Miss Josephine's lovely body. The effrontery of her to stand there in judgment of him with those wide brown eyes—eyes possessed of such clarity that he could see every emotion through them. He almost feared looking into them too deeply.

Worst of all, she had had the audacity to speak to his own reservations where Miss Josephine was concerned.

"Miss Merrill, I leave you to contemplate your situation."

Her eyes widened and pleaded with him.

He could not let her go—did not want to let her go—but could not trust himself to stay. His arousal, hard as the post she was tied to, stretched agonizingly. He turned, avoiding her gaze for fear that he could too easily give in to those doe-like eyes, and left her to seek the reprieve of his own chambers and ponder what the hell he was to do with her next.

* * * * *

Heloise yanked at her bindings with enough desperation to cause the rope to chafe against her wrists. She simply had to escape.

*But escape from what?* a sardonic voice inside her asked. From his exquisite touch? From facing the fact that she had, indeed, enjoyed what he had done to her—that her body had been aroused to wetness by it?

She shook her head vehemently at the voice. Who knew what other devious plans the earl had in store for her? Her backside still smarted from the spanking, which had been utterly mortifying—especially as she had been *aroused* by it. She sensed the danger in her situation. Even now the warmth remained in her loins.

She strained once again at her bonds, her arms sore from their position, and attempted to undo the knot, chipping three of her fingernails in the process. *There simply has to be a way out.*

The door opened and the earl appeared, a touch disheveled but no less dapper. He had removed his coat and loosened his cravat. She stared at the sinews of his throat and felt a wave of warmth washing over her. She quelled it.

"Miss Merrill, I have decided—" he began.

"You will set me free or pay dearly for it," she informed him hotly.

He paused, then raised his brows in amusement—a reaction that only fueled her anger.

"My uncle will see you brought before a magistrate," she continued. "If you do not release me, then prepare to spend your time at Newgate."

He crossed his arms and leaned against the wall. His bemusement when he should have been daunted by her threats both infuriated and worried her.

"On what charges would I be sent to Newgate?" he asked.

*Damn his insolence*, she fumed.

"On kidnapping!" she snapped. "And…and surely there are laws against this…"

"This what, Miss Merrill?"

"You know quite well to what I allude!"

She pulled at her bonds for emphasis, but he continued to wait for her elucidation. She let out a sigh of exasperation.

"Of forcing your attentions upon me!"

To her horror, he laughed. He pulled away from the wall. "Tell me, Miss Merrill, did you not come here of your own free will?"

She bristled. "Yes, but—"

"My coachman was not under orders to abduct anyone."

"Yes, but—"

He took a step toward her. "Did you not lie willingly across my lap?"

Her flush of consternation began to pale.

"You—"

"And requested I spank you four times?"

"I did n—"

"And *enjoyed* it?"

He stood a breath away from her, invading her space and further scattering her thoughts. Her volleys had not struck their target. She needed a new approach.

"How would you explain to a magistrate that you submitted against your will when the evidence reveals your pleasure?"

"Please," Heloise attempted. "Surely you are not without conscience or sensibility…"

"Only devoid of morals," he reminded her.

She swallowed at the verbal blow but pressed on. "You can understand why I might—why I thought I had no other recourse?"

After probing the depths of her gaze he stepped away from her. Without the intrusion of his body, she took an easier breath.

"It is no small effort you have made to protect your cousin's virtue," he acknowledged. "Indeed, you have risked your own ruin to save her."

"I will explain to my family that a dear friend took ill and I went to visit her."

"In the middle of the night? Without packing a valise?"

"I was beside myself."

"I find it hard to believe that Miss Merrill could ever be so discomposed."

"My uncle will have no reason to doubt my word."

"And what of Josephine? What will you tell her?"

"I will beg her forgiveness and hope that she will, in time, come to understand the wisdom of my action."

"Perhaps that will come to pass," he said as he began to walk around her. "Or more likely, she will find another man to whom she can attach her fancy and forget her lost invitation to the Château."

Heloise found herself having to agree with the earl. Nonetheless, she professed, "I hope someone who merits her affection. Someone who will make her happy."

"And what do you hope for yourself, Miss Merrill?"

The question was an unexpected strike. No one had ever asked her that before.

"Myself?"

"What sort of man will you marry or take a fancy to?"

"This is hardly a subject—"

"Pray tell you do not see yourself as a lonely spinster, content after some time to marry a kindly but boring vicar with limited prospects."

That he could guess the precise future she had foreseen for herself disgruntled her.

"That would be better than succumbing to a rake," she retorted.

To her further disconcertion, he laughed. "Do you know what I think, Miss Merrill?"

"I do not *care* what you think, Lord Blythe."

He was standing behind her now—which was worse than when he stood in front of her for now she could not see him. She could only feel his heat.

He leaned toward her. "I think you wanted to come here for yourself. I think if you had been in Josephine's place, you would have accepted my invitation and been furious at anyone who tried to stop you."

Her gaze blurred. She trembled inside. *Good heavens, could it be true?*

\* \* \* \* \*

Stepping toward her, Sebastian lightly grazed the curve of her rump. It proved a mistake. He could breathe in her scent—not the scent of her soap or perfume, but something deeper, something that could best be described as her essence—and it made the blood in him pound. He would have ripped the clothes from her and taken her there against the bedpost if he had lacked the resolve she had so flippantly questioned earlier.

*Hell and damnation.* After having convinced himself in his room earlier that he had provided Miss Merrill a decent set-down, he had returned, prepared to set her free and see her off home. But then she had hurled those threats of hers. And looked so damn delicious tied to the bedpost, still flush with arousal.

For the first time, he had no plan, knew not what he intended. He knew only that his hands itched to touch her, grab her, make her quiver with pleasure.

"Surrender to me."

He knew not from whence the words had come, but suddenly his clothes were too warm. He undid his neckcloth completely.

Silence from her. He considered pressing his erection against her derrière, but he needed her reply. There had been women from whom he sought no consent for he knew full well their desire to be taken. And so he had played the game with them, he the ravisher and they the willing victims.

But not with Miss Merrill. A light spanking was one matter. For what he truly wished to do to her, he wanted her acquiescence. Her submission. Her surrender.

"Surrender yourself," he repeated, softly. "You can trust me."

Though he could not see the expression upon her face, he could sense her defenses coming down. He needed them to come down faster.

"You have such lovely hips, Heloise."

She perked up at the sound of her name and

allowed him to place his hands upon her. He grasped her hips, the flare of which her gown could not hide. What wonderful handles they would provide if he chose to enter her hard from behind.

"And the most delightful rump."

She was likely blushing at the compliment.

He caressed a buttock, then placed his mouth near her ear. "There is so much that can be done here."

He trailed his hand up one side of her arm to her wrist and down the other before cupping a breast. "And here."

A pause. "Such as?"

Ah, he had stimulated her curiosity. Good.

"Anything you wish."

With both hands he manhandled her breasts, eliciting a low groan from her.

"These," he said, "can be fondled, licked, kissed, bitten, suckled…"

Her bosom heaved against his hands.

"Have you had such attentions upon your breasts before, Miss Merrill?"

"No," she murmured.

"Has a man ever taken pleasure from your body?"

He half expected her to rebuke him that such matters were none of his affair, but she replied, "One. There was one."

*One too many*, he thought while impressed, not by the revelation, but by her honesty. Given her obdurate protection of her cousin's virtue, one might expect to find Miss Merrill beyond reproach in regards to her own, but Sebastian knew human fallibility all too well and was relieved to find she was no virgin. That he was not her only encounter roused an unexpected jealousy in his chest. Such a feeling was not common for he had, in the past, often shared his women with the other patrons at Château Follet.

"And did he pleasure you?"

"It was many years ago. We were young."

Just as well she did not answer him directly, Sebastian decided. He was confident he could surpass any experience she might have had and had no desire to know the particulars.

"Then you understand the yearnings of the flesh," he said, sliding his hands down her ribs back to her hips. His fingers slowly gathered her skirts upward. The blood pounded in his head as the image of their naked bodies rutting against the post flashed in his eye. "I may be devoid of morals, but I am no hypocrite."

She stiffened, but he dared hazard her indignation would be short-lived. His fingers continued to lift her skirts.

"Tell me, Miss Merrill, why you find it so depraved to indulge our prurient desires?"

"I don't," she protested. "My censure lies in your seduction of innocent young women."

He did not bother correcting her that it was Josephine who had seduced him, but instead replied, "I willingly engage and seek the companionship of women with similar appetites."

That gave her pause. Apparently it had not occurred to her that he was not the only one guilty of lust. His fingers grazed her thigh as he continued, "I think it immoral of you to impose your sense of morality on others and to deny women the pleasures of the flesh."

"*I* am immoral?" she responded in disbelief. "Because I am not a libertine?"

"Because you would bar fulfillment from others for no purpose."

He slipped his hand between her thighs.

"No purpose, my lord? Protecting a loved one from shame, from risking her future is not reason enough for you?"

He found her clitoris and began a gentle caress. "In whose eyes would she be shamed?"

"Need—need you ask? In the eyes of...polite society."

Her breaths became shallow as he stroked the sensitive nub.

"Setting aside the premise that there is a single pervading norm—which I would dispute—are the darlings of the *beau monde* always right?"

"It matters not if society is right or wrong."

"How convenient," he said ironically, deepening his touch. "What if it were wrong? Ours is a society that once burned people they thought were witches, sanctioned the trading of fellow humans as slaves, governed without representation of the people. By abiding by its norms and following its standards, are you not guilty of supporting its immorality?"

He sensed her thoughts swirling, the wheels of her mind turning, and felt a strange thrill, more exciting than any seduction he had undertaken before. Slipping a finger toward her quim, he discovered her wet with desire. Arousal raged in his pelvis. He was almost there.

"You would believe," she said, still trying to persevere with her own judgment, "that not allowing a woman to become wanton is somehow immoral?"

"Precisely. The suppression of freedom is rarely a good thing. Make no mistake, I do not encourage recklessness or condone any impulse that is criminal. But why should we condemn what are but natural urges of every man and every woman?"

She was gasping as his fingers plied their trade, striking her sensitive spot over and over.

"It may be natural for *you*, my lord."

He fitted his body against hers. Marvelous. The contrast of her soft body against his hardness. With his length, he pushed her into the pole.

"Do you suggest you have no such urges, Miss Merrill?"

He ground his desire into her. Her arms tightened against the pole.

"I do not let such urges overwhelm me."

She clearly knew not what she said for her body indicated otherwise.

"Why not?"

No answer. But her thighs parted for his fingers to conduct their ministrations. He plunged a finger into her quim. She instantly clenched about his digit. He plunged another finger into her as he continued to circle her clitoris with his thumb. She trembled between him and the bedpost, gasping and groaning, groaning and gasping. Her climax loomed near.

"I think, Heloise," he said in a low, husky tone next to her ear, "you should surrender to your natural urges. Allow yourself to indulge in the sublime and submit to me."

Though her body was clearly responding to him, he still wanted to hear her say it. There would be no triumph until she did. When she did not reply, he withdrew his hand. She let out an anguished cry.

"Surrender yourself to me," he tried again.

Her hips ground against him, in search of his hand. He teased her lightly with his fingers, but not enough to make her spend. She moaned.

"Surrender."

Her voice was shaky but the sentence clear.

"Yes…yes, I surrender."

\* \* \* \* \*

An inferno of yearning engulfed her body. Desperate for his touch, for release, Heloise had agreed to submit to the Earl of Blythe. The delectable beginning—of feeling his body pressing hers into the post, of his skilled fingers teasing her body to arousal—had become a divine torture. She felt as if she would go mad if she did not spend, and yet, she exalted in the precipice from which her body dangled. She understood that she *wanted* to submit to him.

And she was not the only one whose desire had been sparked. His erection, hard as stone, pressed against the arch of her arse. That awareness made her cunny ache, made what he did to her all the more pleasing. Her legs threatened to buckle and her arms begged for liberation from their bonds, but she would not give in until she had attained her climax.

She waited for him to resume his stroking. She heard him take a ragged breath. Then felt him step away from her.

*What the bloody…*

She had agreed to surrender to him! Surely he

would reward her now. Her nerves trembled like the vibrations of a tuning fork, seeking the proper conclusion.

*Damnation*, she cursed to herself when still he did nothing. What a fool she was to think that she could expect better from a rake! Had she not accused him of lacking morals? Granted, she knew her statement to have been in the extreme—she suspected he *did* have a conscience or she would have thought all attempts to reason with him hopeless—but he was proving her words now. Well, if he would not help her, she would satisfy herself. She tilted her hips and attempted to grind her mons against the bedpost.

"Stop it," he ordered.

When she refused to obey, he found her nipple and squeezed it. She yelped and stopped.

"You have much to learn, Miss Merrill."

He was back to addressing her formally. She had liked it when he called her 'Heloise.' On his tongue, the name, which she had hitherto found plain, sounded beautiful, inviting and seductive.

Threading his fingers through her hair, he massaged her scalp with both hands, coaxing her resistance away and easing her into a quasi-meditative state. "Have you ever stood naked before a man?" he asked into her ear.

Her heart throbbed, pressing itself against her chest walls as if it had grown too large for its compartment.

There had been an attempt with the son of the squire, but her stays had exasperated the young man. He had thrown her skirts above her waist and penetrated her before prudence, made sluggish by the carnal distress in her own body, could prevail. In the

most unceremonious of minutes she had lost her
virtue. But amidst the aftermath of shame and fear was
a guilty satisfaction, a smugness even, of having
discovered the taboo reserved only for couples
lawfully joined. Having given of herself already, what
was left for her to forsake? Why not indulge her
desires? The experiences of her youth could not
compare to this though, and a part of her yearned to
revel in what might come from a man of
greater…artistry.

"Have you?" he repeated.

"No," she replied.

"You are about to," he informed her, undoing the
back of her gown.

Her pulse quickened. It did not take long for him to
push the top part of her garment off her shoulders and
toward her wrists. He unpinned the skirt and untied
the petticoats. They pooled at her feet. He unlaced her
stays with the swiftness of the most practiced
chambermaid. In little time, she found herself standing
in her chemise, stockings and shoes. Little bumps
lighted her skin at her state of undress. Did he mean to
proceed further? Would she find herself, as he had
suggested, naked before him? What if he did not like
what he saw? He had expected the company of
Josephine, after all.

Reaching around her, he grabbed her breasts
through the chemise. Of a sudden, she yearned to feel
his powerful hands upon her bare flesh. She would
arch her breasts further into his hand were it not for
the post pressing into her sternum. He fingered the
seam of her chemise, and she realized with
embarrassment that she had not selected one of her

finer, less worn undergarments. Fisting the fabric in one hand, he wrenched it against her body.

"Wait!" she gasped. "I haven't—"

Too late. The chemise ripped away from her, scalding the skin where it had most resisted. She took in a sharp breath as if cold had blasted her body, but it was not the air she found chilling. She had no undergarments to wear home. And now she stood with all of her in plain view of his probing eyes—eyes that surely missed little, eyes that were examining every inch of her. What was he thinking? Why did he not speak?

"I will release one of your hands," he told her. "You will pleasure yourself."

Pleasure herself? In front of him? But masturbation was the most private of acts. The notion of touching her genitals before him was horrifying, wicked, and...provocative.

He coaxed her into action with another pinch of her nipple. Her hand flew to her mons and she rubbed two fingers against the little bud nestled between her folds. It was awkward with the bedpost in the way. She had to arch her derrière to provide her hand enough access. At first she felt only shame. There was nothing pleasurable about fondling herself before Lord Blythe. He had sauntered to the side for a better view. But when she chanced to meet his smoldering gaze, saw the slight ripple of muscle above his jaw, desire flamed in her loins. She rubbed herself more purposefully, making the anticipation quiver down the length of her legs.

He went to stand behind her once more and,

reaching around her hip, he joined his hand to hers between her thighs. Their fingers bumped against each other. The agitation blazing in her body was ten times stronger than what she had felt earlier. She did not care if he ordered her to stop this time. She would not do it. Her body deserved to spend this time.

And spend it did. She jerked against the post as her wave crested, rolling her beneath it, into the glorious turbulence of release. It flared deep in her groin, shot down her legs. A wrenching cry tore from her throat. When at last she surfaced for air, she felt weak and ragged. Her legs collapsed beneath her just as he swept her into his arms and undid the cord that bound her one arm to the bedpost. He tossed aside the bodice of her gown and laid her across the bed.

With her eyes closed to contain the intensity of sensations that had just assaulted her, she breathed in the relief of her accomplishment, her body satisfied and content. He caressed her thighs, her hips, her waist.

"Well done, Heloise."

"Mmmmm," she acknowledged, relishing the sound of her name upon his tongue.

She thought he might now put his triumph into words, and she would not have cared much if he did. Lord Blythe had known somehow that she had wanted this. To attempt denials now would prove a futile exercise. But he said nothing. Instead of proclaiming victory—she expected some level of smugness from a man as arrogant as he—he had praised her. His gentle touch lulled into her a state of peaceful bliss but a gradual arousal also began to build. She could feel the curve of his body behind hers. She was becoming sensitized to him in the most alarming and thrilling ways. How was it he could awaken her body with the simplest of caresses? Wetness pooled between her legs once again, desire welling in her veins. She hoped that he would touch her more intimately.

Just as she was about to beg ask, his hand circled around her thigh, grazed the soft curls at her mons, and reached for the supple folds below. She could hardly wait to see what he would do next.

\* \* \* \* \*

Sebastian was not surprised at how well Miss Merrill had spent. Wild thoughts ran through his head at the possibilities. There was so much he could do to her. So much he wanted to do to her besides fondle her against the bedpost. Containing the force of his lust had been like pushing a coach and four up a steep slope, but after she had finished convulsing against the bedpost, when he knew the soreness in her arm would come alive with a vengeance, a flood of tenderness had filled him. The sense of satisfaction as he cradled her in his arms was greater than he could ever remember it being. He knew not why he felt such a strong desire to protect her.

And claim her as his.

Marguerite had been surprised by Miss Merrill, but no more surprised than he. He had taken dozens of women far comelier and more practiced than Miss Merrill. How was it then that he felt driven to madness by her? A cautionary bell rang in his head, one that questioned the wisdom of pursuing anything further.

Her coiffure had mostly come undone, and tendrils

of hair curled about her face and down her neck. Tiny beads of perspiration dotted her nose. He liked her look of disarray. Liked that he was the one who had placed her in such a state. The flush in her rounded cheeks added to her loveliness. His hand wound its way to her mons, brushing her curls and feeling for the dampness between her thighs. A soft moan escaped her lips when he brushed past her clitoris.

He nibbled her ear. "Tell me now, Heloise, how you enjoyed your surrender."

"I suppose rather well," she murmured.

*Impudent chit*, Sebastian thought to himself. He plunged his fingers into her wet folds and jarred them against a raised area of nerves.

"Ahhh," she gasped.

"Only 'rather well'?"

"Extremely well—much—I much enjoyed it."

*That is better.* He pressed his groin against her buttocks as his fingers continued their assault. She arched herself into his hands.

"Do you desire more, Miss Merrill?"

Without pause, she nodded. "Say it."

"I wish for more."

"More what?"

"More of what you would do to me, my lord."

"Do you wish me to fondle you with my fingers?"

"Mmmm."

"Take you fully?"

Her eyes flew open. Lust smoldered in her countenance.

"Yes, " she answered in no uncertain terms.

This time it was he who groaned. With one hand still trapped between her thighs, he tore the buttons of his fall loose with the other. His erection sprang out, famished for contact. Too impatient to pull his pants down, he glided his cock between her legs from behind, then slid an arm beneath her.

He reminded her, "If you are uncertain, you have but to say—"

"Yes, yes," she interrupted. "Be a gentleman and pray do not keep a lady waiting."

He ought to reprove her for her audacity, but he hungered too much for her at the moment. Without ceremony, he plunged himself into her. She cried out in shock as most, but not all, of his length filled her. Sebastian closed his eyes and took in a deep breath, longing to push himself deeper but wanting her to adjust to the sudden invasion. He knew not how long it had been since last she had been filled. His fingers played her clitoris while the other hand grabbed a breast.

She flexed against his hardness. He sank himself deeper into her wet and glorious heat. Suddenly, it wasn't enough for him to be pulsing deep inside of her. An insatiable desire to have his body completely merged with hers took hold. He grabbed her chin and turned her mouth toward his, then clamped his lips to hers. At last. How supple, how yielding her lips felt. And he plumbed the depths of her mouth as vigorously as he would plumb the depths of her quim.

She attempted to return his kiss, but he was too busy tasting her, feeling her with his tongue, taking in her air, breathing in her essence. His mouth worked her over, and he felt a rush of her hot liquid encasing his cock. When he finally pulled his mouth from hers, her breath was heavy and she looked dazed. Perhaps he had been a little too fierce in his kiss. He knew not the source of this unexpected ferocity, but he had to sample her mouth once more.

Muffling whatever she was about to say, he pressed his mouth hard to hers. He kissed and sucked her until her lips swelled with lust and the lines of her mouth flushed from the attention. It was maddening, this dueling desire between his mouth and his cock. But the grinding of her hips against him recalled the arousal between his legs. Slowly, he pulled his cock out. She moaned as his shaft grazed her engorged nub of desire. He plunged back into her and closed his eyes to concentrate. His sac boiled, greedy for release. A tremor threatened the control of his legs.

She let out a delicious cry as he plunged himself back in. He returned a hand between her legs and began a rhythmic thrusting.

"Oh, *God*," she pleaded, circling her arms behind her and wrapping them about his neck.

A mirror strategically placed opposite them showed two bodies, one darker than the other, writhing in unison, their purpose common. The light of the candles flickered a warm inviting glow upon her milky skin. Her tousled hair was damp about her face from perspiration. He saw his hand fondling her breast. Despite the hardness of her nipples, her areolas remained large, dark discs. He captured the vision of her, of them, in his mind. The image fueled the rage in his cock, and he began to pound her as his fingers plied her with increasing energy and speed.

"Oh God, oh God, oh God," she cried before a scream split their grunting sounds and her body spasmed violently against him.

He continued to piston in and out of her until he had wrung the last of her orgasm out of her. And then he succumbed to the needs of his own body. The scalding desire roiling in his abdomen exploded out his cock, blending into her wetness. With a roar he pumped himself into her. Her body was his. Meant to serve his desires now.

Tremors shot down his legs as his climax peaked. He did not realize how hard he was squeezing her breast until she cried out. He let go and wrapped her in his arms as his lust finished draining into her. The blood pounded relentlessly in his head, but he managed to kiss her gently on the temple. She nestled closer to him. This too was glorious.

And as he cradled her in his arms, he found himself wishing that what she had said was true. He wished he was indeed devoid of morals.

# CHAPTER THREE

Heloise awoke to find Lord Blythe gone. At first his disappearance did not trouble her. The pleasure of her experience still lingered and as she stretched her arms overhead, she recalled as much as she could, not wanting her memory to forget the smallest detail. Strange as it seemed, it was not merely the havoc he had wreaked upon her body—she had never thought her body could react as intensely as it had—that she cherished the most. The overwhelming sense of freedom, of trust, was what had elevated her experience to the heavens.

She also recalled with fondness their dialogue. That was how he had seduced her. Despite her belief that his philosophy was self-serving—it had to be, for how could someone genuinely believe such radical liberalism?—she had found their conversation stimulating. And he seemed perfectly at ease having such a discussion with her when others would have scoffed at her as some blue stocking. Thus, she did not mind that he might have proved her a hypocrite. She would be more than content to have him prove the point over and over again.

Annabelle appeared at the door with a tray. "His lordship asked me to bring some victuals."

Eying the thinly sliced ham and colorful sweetmeats, Heloise realized she was famished. Annabelle set the tray upon the bed and poured a glass of wine.

"Your gown is being ironed, madam," Annabelle said, "and I shall return shortly to attend to your toilette."

"Thank you."

After a quick bob, the maid left. As Heloise buttered her bread, she wondered why she should bother getting dressed if she would end up naked again. Oh, but the process of undressing was delightful. She wondered if she would have the opportunity to see him completely naked. The thought made her salivate more than the food.

"The berries are fresh from the garden."

She glanced quickly to the door. The Earl of Blythe stood on the threshold, dressed magnificently in gray. She had never found gray to be an appealing color, but he wore it well. The hue would have made a pale man look ashen but did nothing to tarnish the bronze in Lord Blythe's complexion. He wore his riding hat and riding boots and a light cloak was draped about his shoulders.

"Are you headed out?" she asked. She glanced out the windows to see that the sun had just begun to emerge from the horizon.

"If you leave within the hour, you will be home not long after dawn," he informed her.

Her brows lifted in reaction—she had not even

been here a day—but the tone of his voice suggested he had no interest in prolonging her stay. What had happened? Had she done something to offend? She had thought he approved of her performance. Was that not so?

"You're letting me go?" she asked.

"It was never my intention to keep you prisoner. I may be devoid of morals, but I am no tyrant."

Never his intention or not his desire? Would he have felt differently if she were Josephine?

"What of Josephine?" she inquired when he touched his hat to her and prepared to take his leave.

"You may rest easy, Miss Merrill. I will not be extending another invitation to your cousin."

Because he might end up with her instead? She watched him depart in stunned silence. Was this how he was with the other women? Did he bring them ecstasy, show them a bit of affection, then cast them aside as quickly as possible?

Of course. What a fool she had been to think that he might have taken a fancy to her. Apparently she did not merit even a full weekend with him. He had proved his point and shown her for a charlatan. Did she expect anything else from entangling herself with a rake like Sebastian Cadwell?

The bread, though freshly baked, suddenly tasted stale to her. With a sigh, she pushed away the tray and rose from the bed to prepare for a long and lonely journey home.

\* \* \* \* \*

"Surely you are not leaving so soon, *mon cheri?*"

Lady Follet asked from the settee where she lounged in a stola.

Sebastian bowed. "I have no reason to stay, and came only to bid you *adieu*."

"*Adieu*? But why?" Marguerite persisted as she plucked a grape off its stem.

He eyed the two brawny men, dressed in togas, who had been servicing her. "I have no wish to trouble you with more than a goodbye, seeing as you are occupied, my lady."

She waved her pair of Adonises away. "I am now *un*occupied."

"Nevertheless, I intend a brief farewell."

Marguerite pursed her lips in a pout. He could not help but compare her wide and thin lips with those of Miss Merrill's. Parting from Miss Merrill had proved more difficult than he had anticipated—especially as she sat naked in that bed. He had considered taking her one last time, but that would only have delayed the inevitable awkwardness. And he had had a hard enough time looking into her eyes after what had transpired between them.

"Ah, you offended your lady friend in some manner and she is leaving in a huff," Marguerite noted. "You will, of course, give chase, prove that she cannot resist you, and ravish her madly in your carriage."

He swallowed hard, trying not to imagine the scene being played out with Heloise—Miss Merrill.

"I am sending her away," he explained.

"But why?"

"Because she came in error. She is not suited for Château Follet."

"Her cries would indicate otherwise. She was enjoying herself—my servants told me they could hear her from down the hall. And, regardless of what Anne Wesley would say, no woman has been known to be dissatisfied in your hands."

Sebastian let out an impatient breath through his nose. He had little desire to discuss the matter with Marguerite, but she was the hostess, and his manners would not allow him to dismiss her easily.

"The misgivings lie with me."

"She displeased you."

He wished that were the case. He wished that he had not found her courage and attempts at boldness endearing. Nor her vulnerability so alluring. Her body so intoxicating.

"She pleased me well enough."

Marguerite arched her brows. "Pray tell you are not developing a conscience, *mon cheri?*"

Women. They could be damnably clever at the most inconvenient times.

"She would not think it possible," he replied wryly, "having denounced me as a libertine devoid of morals."

"But why would she...? Strange words for a woman who came here to experience the pleasures of the flesh."

Sebastian could see Marguerite would not relent until she understood the situation. Only women had such propensities.

"She did not come here to indulge her carnal desires," he divulged, "but to rescue her cousin from ruin at my hands. Her cousin was my intended guest."

"*Mon dieu.* She took her cousin's place? What a

peculiar mademoiselle."

He took this opportunity to raise her hand to his lips. "And now, my dear, I bid you a fond farewell, until next we meet."

She pulled her hand away before he could kiss it. "But you—you seduced her?"

He felt a muscle ripple along his jaw. "My dear, I see no purpose in furthering this *tête-à-tête*. My horse has been saddled."

He turned to leave but was stopped again by her words.

"But why stop now? Why send her away? Does she want to leave?"

"Why so many questions about her?" he retorted. "Why, of the many women who have been through Château Follet, does she merit such curiosity?"

"Because she's not like the many women who have been here. At least not the ones you have brought."

"I did not bring her. She came uninvited."

"Nonetheless, you enjoyed her, did you not?"

Hostess or no, Lady Follet was about to have a rude guest on her hands, he thought to himself.

"It makes little sense that you are sending her away so soon," Marguerite continued, "lest it be an act of conscience, of some form of chivalry. And so, my dear Sebastian, I may ask of you—why her?"

"She is no jezebel. She deserves better."

She stared blankly at him, and he thought that he might finally have put an end to the conversation, but then she began to laugh. Containing his irritation, he waited patiently for her to be done with the hilarity.

"Forgive me," she said at last, wiping away a tear. "I never would have thought to hear you utter such things, but I rather suspected that the day would come when a woman would stir the tender part of you."

The choice of weapon for women was words, and Marguerite, like Miss Merrill, would have done as well had she kicked him in the groin.

"I am pleased to be a source of humor for you, my dear, but I fail to see where this dialogue is headed."

"*Mon dieu*, I have never seen you this cross. This mademoiselle must be *très special*, indeed. I must meet her."

He took a step toward her. "You will not."

Her brows shot up. "How protective we are. Tell me, she did not ask for you to send her away?"

"It matters not."

"Of course it does. You said she deserved better. What if she doesn't want better—at the least, not your patronizing definition of what is better for her."

He considered Marguerite's words and tried to recall Miss Merrill's reaction upon hearing that she was to return home. He had been so immersed in his own objective that he had not paid much attention to what she might have been thinking.

"It is better that she go," he said at last.

"Coward."

Of all the things Marguerite could have said, he did not expect that. Rather, he had thought she might praise him for his rare display of chivalry with Miss Merrill or chastise him for being a chivalrous prude. Being called a coward was worse than anything Anne Wesley might have said.

"My dear, you are deliberately trying to provoke my ire," he said, taking off his gloves as if he meant to slap her across the face and challenge her to a duel.

She eyed the gloves warily. "Only because I adore you, Sebastian, and only the friendship between us stays the jealousy I feel towards your mademoiselle."

"If you wish to renew our acquaintance, I can have the groom unsaddle my horse."

"No. I will not serve as a means for you to forget *her*. I do not wish for you to envision her while you lie with me. If you are the Sebastian Cadwell I thought you were, you would not let her go."

"How many times do you intend to challenge my manhood, Marguerite?"

She smiled.

"It would do no good," he said. "If she returns home now, there is a chance no one would find out that she had ever been here. If she stayed, while we might enjoy ourselves for a few days more, we would only defer the misery of parting."

"That has never stopped you before. Is it her misery or yours that concerns you?"

He considered the many women he had bid farewell to. Some parted with wistfulness, others parted with vain attempts to seduce him. But he had been clear with them all—their time at Château Follet marked the end and not the beginning of an affair. He did not think he could bear seeing the sadness in Miss Merrill's eyes. Already he suspected she, like so many before her, had fallen a little in love with him. Nor had he a desire to enlarge the emptiness he was already feeling upon her departure.

"I will not see her ruined," he said stubbornly.

"How condescending of you."

Her words struck him as ironic. He had used the same with Miss Merrill. And now it was he who sought to shield her from herself—contradicting his own arguments. He would have preferred to keep Miss Merrill and show her body the many paths to ecstasy. Instead, he had chosen to be selfless, and for that he was being called a condescending coward.

"Go to her, *mon cheri*," Marguerite urged.

She gazed at him with obvious affection. He wondered if Miss Merrill would gaze at him with such warmth. The prospect beckoned as much as her body called to his.

"*Adieu*, my dear," he said to Marguerite with a kiss to her forehead.

And this time, before she could utter another objection, he took his leave.

\* \* \* \* \*

Heloise had the carriage deposit her a mile from the Merrill estate with the intention of traversing the remaining distance on foot. Watching the carriage withdrawing into the sunset, she was poignantly conscious that her assignation with Lord Blythe was over. She might not cross paths again with him for some time, and she would prefer the absence to the inevitable awkwardness that must accompany future encounters between them.

She welcomed the solitary walk, hoping the pleasant glow of dusk would calm her unrest. Cadwell had stirred an agitation within her that she could not quiet. Longing for his touch, her body felt as though it were a tuning fork that could not cease its reverberation. What a muddle she had made of herself! Though driven by good intentions, she had succeeded in accomplishing nothing save making a proper fool of herself before the Earl of Blythe. Her cheeks flushed at what he must think of her now.

The most troubling aspect of it all was that she cared what he thought.

As she approached the house, her thoughts turned to Josephine and the dreaded confrontation. How would she explain herself to her cousin? She had reconciled herself to the prospect of losing Josephine's affection in exchange for "rescuing" her cousin from Lord Blythe, but now that her mission had proved a failure—and that she herself had succumbed to that from which she had sought to protect Josephine—she no longer felt secure in her standing.

"Miss Merrill!" the maidservant at the door greeted her in surprise, louder than Heloise would have liked. "We was in quite a state as to where you might have gone off to."

"I went to call upon an ailing friend," Heloise mumbled as she glanced about for her cousin with a quickened pulse. "Where is Miss Josephine?"

"In the garden, I believe, with Mr. Webster."

Mr. Webster was a friend of Lord Blythe and had called once before on Josephine.

"Is anyone else with them?"

The maid shook her head. Heloise sighed at Josephine's disregard for a chaperone, but she was relieved too, that she might not have to confront her cousin quite yet.

"Shall I assist in your toilette, Miss Merrill?"

With her skirts dust-covered from the walk, Heloise realized she must have looked rather unkempt from her travels. They went upstairs to her chambers, which now looked a tad drab compared to those at the Château Follet.

As she unlaced her bonnet and shrugged out of her caraco, she thought once again of Lord Blythe, of his hands undressing her, his body pressed against her. How quickly her apprehension had transformed to comfort in his presence, as if they had been lovers for some time. "Allow me."

Heloise whirled around. She had stepped out of her skirts and awaited the maid to unlace her stays when Josephine appeared. Her breath stalled.

Josephine pulled at the ribbons without word. The frown upon her lips and the stiffness of her hand revealed her displeasure. "You know?" Heloise ventured.

"I was awaiting the invitation. When none arrived and I discovered you absent without any of the servants knowing your whereabouts, I suspected your interference."

She forced a breath. "Forgive me, Josephine."

Josephine paused before replying, her voice quavering with anger, "You are not my keeper, Heloise."

Heloise stared at the floor. "I know. I was wrong to have intervened. I should not censure you were you to decide never to speak to me again."

"Then why did you?" her cousin accused.

Noble if not condescending sentiments, the earl had said.

Heloise took a deep breath and looked into Josephine's eyes. "I was a fool."

With an exasperated sigh, Josephine flopped into

an armchair nearby. "You went all the way to Château Follet?"

She nodded.

"And spoke with Lord Blythe?"

"Yes."

"What did you say to him?"

"I beseeched him not to besmirch your honor."

Josephine snorted. "What did he say?"

"That I was intolerant and that you were not in leading strings."

Her cousin pursed her lips as silence fell between them. Heloise had stepped out of her stays and clasped her hands together. She had prepared herself for Josephine's wrath and was ready to receive it.

"That is not your chemise," Josephine observed with narrowed eyes.

Heloise eyed the undergarment with its lace edging. It was more exquisite than any she owned and belonged to Lady Follet. However, Lady Follet had a slender figure and the chemise stretched visibly over Heloise's body. She searched her mind for a reasonable explanation but contrived nothing. Now Josephine would be livid...

"What happened at the château, Heloise?"

Her mouth opened, but no words emerged. Helpless and embarrassed, she could only look at Josephine stupidly.

"Heloise, did you and Lord Blythe...?"

She dropped her gaze and felt her cheeks redden.

Josephine shook her head. "That rake! I wonder that he accepted you for a replacement?"

Heloise looked at her cousin. "I am sure he was exceedingly disappointed."

Silence. Then a sly smile pulled at the corner of Josephine's mouth. "Well, Heloise. I must say that such display of boldness on your part is quite surprising!"

"I will no longer attempt to thwart your acquaintance with him," Heloise assured her.

Josephine sniffed. "Indeed! Imagine what would be said of you if it should be discovered you spent the night at Château Follet. I think you shall no longer lord over me simply because you are my senior. But did Lord Blythe make mention of when he would repair my stolen invitation?"

A shameful seed of jealousy threatened to sprout, but Heloise suppressed the feeling. "He did not."

Josephine knit her brows for a moment, but then waved a hand dismissively. "The invitation is no great loss, though admittedly, I was quite furious when it dawned on me what you had done. But if the Earl of Blythe will not replicate the invitation to Château Follet, *Mr. Webster* will."

Heloise said nothing.

"Tell me, is Lord Blythe as divine as rumored?"

*And more*, Heloise thought. She noted the mischievous sparkle in her cousin's eye.

"He is!" Josephine exclaimed. "For you are blushing as scarlet as a pimpernel."

"Only because I have made a royal fool of myself. He proved me for a hypocrite."

"I own it is a relief to find you are not quite so virtuous. It is rather taxing to think that I am somehow short of character when compared to you."

Heloise let out a shaky breath. "I think that I owe you my confidence, dear cousin, but I was compromised long before this."

Josephine's eyes turned into saucers.

"Of my own volition," Heloise added. "Perhaps that is why I thought it no large matter to…to lie with Lord Blythe."

"And I had been led to believe you were the virtuous one!"

"When your father was kind enough to take me in, I vowed I would not bring shame upon him—or you, Josephine. You are my only family and far too dear to me."

"But you ought not advise me to adhere to expectations you yourself have not fulfilled."

"Your prospects, Josephine, are much greater than mine."

"Yes, yes, but it is so much more pleasurable to succumb."

Heloise sighed in agreement. She sat down on the bed, and the two shared a moment of silence.

"There is no purpose in protecting me, Heloise. I had surrendered my maidenhead a year ago."

Now it was Heloise's turn to be surprised. "Of your own volition? Did you consider the consequences?"

"Did you?" Josephine retorted.

"Touché."

"Where is the harm if no one knows?"

"I wish we had shared our confidences earlier. Perhaps all this could have been avoided."

"Perhaps. But then you would not have experienced the embrace of Lord Blythe."

Heloise thought of the desire that had been stoked to life by the earl. The hunger had lain dormant these years—suppressed—and she had lamented its awakening at first. But perhaps she could exalt in its vigor instead? Why should the thrill of it turn sour simply because she could not be with Lord Blythe?

Looking at her cousin, she saw that Josephine's countenance had softened. "I hope that someday you may forgive me, Josephine."

"I may be cross with you still," Josephine said, but a faint smile tugged at one corner of her lips. "But I do prefer the Heloise I know now."

Heloise felt as if a boa had loosened its hold of her chest.

Josephine leaned in. "Now tell me *everything* about the Château Follet..."

\* \* \* \* \*

Closing his eyes, Sebastian imagined the plush lips of Heloise Merrill, her mouth waiting to be plumbed by his. He had taken notice of her mouth ever since their encounter at the theater, when her bottom lip had dropped in astonishment over something he had said. He had been tempted then to run his thumb over her succulent lips. He saw himself thrusting into her, saw her eyes bright with desire as she returned his gaze.

The stream of his desire shot from him as the screams of the woman beneath him jolted him from his reverie.

He climbed off her before the last of his seed had emptied. Stumbling, he leaned against the wall for support and took in a deep breath. He was not in the Empress Room of Château Follet but the boudoir of an opera dancer, and the woman sprawled upon the bed with her skirts thrown above her waist was not

Miss Merrill but a woman whose name he could barely recall. Three days had passed since he had left the château and still he could not quiet the humming in his body whenever he thought of Miss Merrill. Perhaps he should not have dismissed her quite so soon from Château Follet. There was much he wanted to show her, much he wanted to do with her body. He wondered which position he would most favor with her—throwing her legs over his shoulders, pressing her against the wall, or taking her from behind as she knelt on all fours?

The answer would surely prove to be *all of them*.

Despite having just spent, he felt desire welling once more in his groin. He glanced at the woman, now asleep, in the bed before him. For a moment he considered climbing back onto her, but she looked far too tranquil in her slumber, and he suspected that pounding himself senselessly into her would not dispel his thoughts of Miss Merrill.

An hour later he found himself at Brooks's, but neither cards nor drink proved an effective distraction. He longed not only for her body but her company. There was so little he knew of her, save that Jonathan Merrill had become her guardian upon the death of her parents. He wanted to know what she thought of Château Follet after her experience with him? He would like to believe that he had surpassed the depths of any encounters she had had with her previous lover.

*"Go to her,"* Marguerite had urged.

He imagined the possibilities of a second encounter with Miss Merrill. The grounds of the château possessed a bucolic charm, and he would have liked to take her on a stroll and engage her in a less confrontational situation. He sensed that he could speak to her as a peer and on a world of topics. Some women had a most annoying practice of feigning ignorance or appearing stupid to please the vanity of the men in their company, but Heloise was as likely to challenge him. Of course he could always silence any argument from her by smothering her mouth with his own.

A second assignation would provide him an opportunity to make amends for his abrupt departure from her. The look of surprise, the slight frown of her brows had indicated her disappointment when he had taken his leave. He had no doubt she had the fortitude to recover, though he half wished, selfishly, that her recovery would not be too swift. He wondered if he occupied her thoughts as much as she did his. He hoped, for her sake, that it would not be the case. Or did he?

He shook his head. He had denied his lust in favor of honor. To seek another meeting with Heloise would tarnish the integrity of his *noblesse oblige*. There were others more suited to Château Follet. Perhaps he could amuse himself by seducing Anne Wesley into retracting her unkind words. He was confident she would sing his praises before long.

Time would ensure that Miss Merrill became but a faint memory. If only that were what he desired.

\* \* \* \* \*

The weeds resisted, and Heloise welcomed their defiance as she tugged at them—anything to command her attention and keep her mind off Château

Follet and the Earl of Blythe. A sennight had passed and still it was no easy matter to forget him, especially in the quiet of night. Lying in bed, she would caress the parts of her that he had caressed. Her body longed for his touch and the way he made her feel alive. She missed their exchanges.

But she had not heard from him since leaving Château Follet. She knew not if he had attempted to contact Josephine. Somehow she suspected he was done with both Miss Merrill as well as Miss Josephine.

The afternoon sun shone brightly and perspiration trickled down the side of her face as her uncle approached her. He looked very much like her father, only a bit more stout about the belly. She often thought how fortunate she was that she had such a kindhearted guardian.

"Er, Heloise," he said, peering at her through his bifocals. He hesitated, apparently deciding not to say what he had initially intended.

Ceasing her activity, Heloise looked up at him and waited.

After clearing his throat a few times, her uncle blurted, "How do you know the Earl of Blythe?"

Heloise felt her stomach drop. "Sir?"

"He is not a man I thought would be familiar to you."

Avoiding his gaze, Heloise wondered how she could answer him. This was not how she had meant to repay his kindness for taking her in, and yet she was guilty of deception and shame. Should she confess the whole truth and offer to take her leave? Surely he would not want to keep her in his household after learning the truth?

"He has a…" her uncle began again, "a repute of sorts, you know."

"Yes, I am aware of his character," she replied, fidgeting with her gloves. She dug for courage to ask, "Why do you wish to speak of Lord Blythe?"

"He is here."

Her breath halted sharply. "He—Lord Blythe came to see you?"

"He came not for me but for you."

"Me?" she echoed. "Not…Josephine?"

"He was quite clear. A direct man, the earl. In truth, his candor took me by surprise. Nonetheless, I told him that I would not be deemed a responsible guardian if I were to countenance your acquaintance with him. He said he quite understood my fear that I would be feeding the sheep to the wolf, as it were, but he praised your sense of judgment, and I had to agree. I do wish Josephine shared of your discrimination."

The irony of his words made her cringe.

"I leave it up to you then," he continued, "to decide if you will see him. If you've no wish to, I will send him away."

Heloise searched his face and realized there was no anger there.

"I will see him."

When her uncle left, she wished she had asked him to make the earl wait in the drawing room, that she might have an opportunity to attend her toilette. Having exerted some effort in gardening, she must have looked as unkempt as she had that first day at Madame Follet's. She removed her gloves, wiped the perspiration from her brow, and attempted to tuck her curls into some sense of order.

But why worry of her appearance? she reasoned to herself. She knew not the purpose of his call. Indeed, she had not expected to see him again after his departure from the château. But perhaps he harbored some guilt for having seduced her? Or wished to point out that he had not seduced her but that she had willingly given herself to him so that she had no claims upon his conscience? Perhaps he wished once more to warn her not to meddle in his affairs. Well, she had no intention of interfering in his pursuit of her cousin. And she had no wish to force his hand. No one knew she was ruined, and she trusted him not to speak of it. Though she had not been able to refrain from thinking of him these past days, he would not know it.

Still, she could not stay her vanity from smoothing down her gown and being dismayed upon discovering a stain. She tried to rub it out.

"Miss Merrill."

Her head snapped up to see the Earl of Blythe standing before her, as immaculately dressed as ever in his high polished Hessians, trim cutaway coat with brass buttons and starched cravat.

"Your lordship," Heloise returned as blandly as she could, attempting not to be unnerved by the manner in which his gaze bored into her as she bobbed a curtsy.

Silence settled between them as he took her in. Heloise pulled at the fingers of her gloves. It was he who had called upon her. Why did he not speak? Afraid that he would unearth her true feelings, she kept her eyes averted and waited unsuccessfully for him to begin the dialogue. When he did not, she was tempted to ask him if he had come all this way simply to stare at her.

"You have a purpose for your visit, Lord Blythe?" she relented at last.

He eyed her carefully. "Indeed."

The man was insufferable. He was not making this easy for her.

"My cousin is not here," she informed him, tossing her gloves into a basket with her gardening tools. She was determined that he would not know the pain she had felt when he had left the château with only the slightest by-your-leave. Nor would he know the anger she felt—anger that now fueled her nerves when a part of her wanted only to flee from him that she might shed her tears in solitude.

"I came not for her."

Of course she knew that. Her uncle had said as much. Nonetheless, and though she knew not the purpose of his call, she felt gratified to hear from his own lips that he was here for her, no matter his purpose.

"Then why did you come?" she ventured.

"Our farewell at the château was unsatisfactory," he answered, his voice dark.

Ah. She had suspected he had more compassion than he had shown.

"I found it decent enough," she lied and even managed a small smile at him. Her response seemed to unsettle him, but her triumph was diminished by the wretchedness she felt. She wished he would leave so that she might properly grieve over a romance that lived only in her imagination, berate herself for having been such a dolt, and return to being the sensible young woman her uncle had praised but moments ago.

A sensible and wiser woman.

He narrowed his eyes. "It was an abrupt *adieu*."

"It was." She considered as she picked up her basket, proud that she maintained her composure, but she did not trust it to last much longer. "But pray do not trouble yourself on that."

She turned to leave but he grasped her wrist. Her heart hammered violently at his touch.

"Trouble myself?" he said in a near growl. "I have only slept fitfully these last seven nights since leaving you."

For the first time she noticed the darkness beneath his eyes. Had he as strong a conscience as that? Despite her anger at him, her heart ached for his distress.

When he did not release her, she glanced toward the house to see if her uncle might be watching. He would not approve of such familiarity from the earl. Realizing the same, Lord Blythe dropped her wrist— reluctantly, it seemed.

"It were my own fault," he said. "It was not a proper farewell."

Though his jaw was still tight, the look in his eyes had softened. She faltered and could not stop her voice from quavering as she asked, "What…what would you have considered a proper farewell, my lord?"

His gaze made the space about them intimate without his having to stir. His response was low and husky. "Something I dare not do at present, for I would not cause a scandal in your uncle's garden."

She stared at him with her mouth agape. Groaning, he glanced toward the house, then defiantly stepped toward her, placed his finger beneath her chin as he had done that night in the theater, and closed her mouth.

"Your lips will be the death of me, Miss Merrill," he murmured.

The hammering of her heart moved up into her head, making it difficult for her to think. His touch recalled their night of passion, and her body thrilled to it instantly. In his eyes, she now beheld a smoldering agony. Did she dare hope…?

"My lips?"

"Yes. The vision of which has haunted me day and night."

She closed her eyes and heard his words echo in her head. *Haunted me day and night.* Just as he had haunted her thoughts and dreams. The anguish melted from her and with it her calm.

A breeze wafted around them, blowing the scent of the flowers into the air.

As if encouraged by the look in her eyes when she opened them, Sebastian continued, "I came, Miss Merrill, to inform your uncle of my intentions to court you."

Dumbfounded, she could only stare at him. The words he had uttered sounded almost ludicrous. Court her?

"I intend the courtship to bear all the markings of respectability," he assured her, unsettled by her silence, "though, damn me, it will be no easy feat when my body burns with desire for you."

Her mouth fell open again. If her heart could glow, she would be brighter than a beacon. She recovered from the audacity of his statement. "Respectability from you, Lord Blythe?"

"It took me seven days to realize that I have no choice but to attempt respectability if I ever hope to possess you in my arms once more. You deserve no less. But I give you fair warning—you know me for what I am, Miss Merrill."

"I do not think I do," she returned. "I thought our affair confined to the château. Your departure made that quite clear, I think."

"I was appalled," he explained, "that you might be discovered in a compromising situation."

She flushed. "You may recall, sir, that you have not the honor of having been the first."

A muscle rippled along his jaw. "I will not discuss the particulars of *that*. I thought that you would wake with remorse for what had happened betwixt us and that you would be relieved for me to be gone."

"Yet here you are," she pointed out.

"Yes, here am I, for it is the nature of the male sex to pursue, against all odds, until he has been bludgeoned and all recourse dissolved. I want you, Miss Merrill, more than I have ever wanted most other women. If the nature of such feelings should be love, I will not spurn it."

She contemplated what he said, her gaze raking over him, saying nothing. She felt mastery of the situation, for he had made clear his feelings but she had yet to reveal hers. He was staring at her as if she were prey he meant to devour. Desire lighted his eyes, and the look made her loins warm and a familiar wetness begin to form. But she continued playing the coquette through her silence for well he deserved it.

"You disappointed me, Lord Blythe," she said at last.

His brows rose.

"I had hoped to stay the full three nights at Lady Follet's," she finished.

He beamed.

"As for respectability..." she continued, her eyes bright as she leaned toward him, "that sounds rather boring."

He groaned. "Miss Merrill, you would make a further rake of me."

"There is a part of the garden hidden from all view," she whispered with a sly smile.

"I could not, Miss Merrill," he said after some hesitation. "I may be a rake, but you will not find it so easy to question my resolve as you had. I will be a gentleman."

*Not for long*, she thought to herself. She had no qualms about seducing him. But she gave him her brightest smile and took the arm he offered to escort her back to the house.

"How unfortunate," she replied lightly, using his words. "Perhaps that can be changed."

The Earl of Blythe grinned. "My dear Miss Merrill, you are a perfect rake."

## THE END

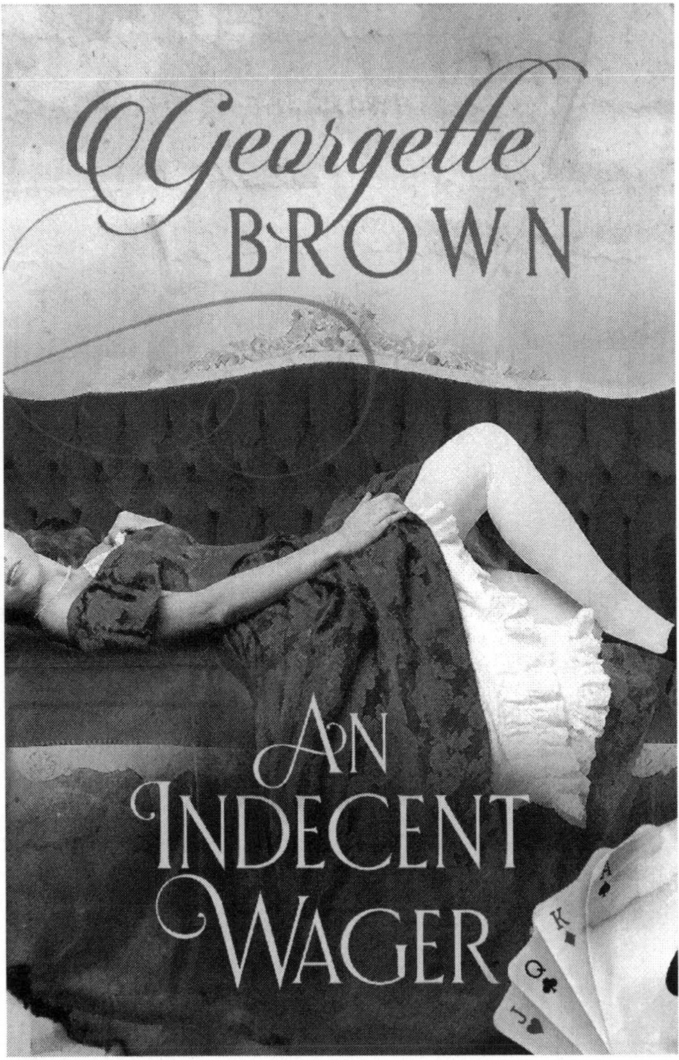
Georgette
BROWN
AN
INDECENT
WAGER

# AN INDECENT
# WAGER

# CHAPTER ONE

Deana could muster no oath strong enough to reflect the dismay she felt when Lord Halsten Rockwell revealed his ace and queen. She glanced at her own cards, a king and a ten, to ascertain she had indeed lost. How was it possible? Rockwell had been losing all night.

"You owe me fifty pounds, Miss Herwood," Lord Rockwell stated placidly as he collected the winnings in the middle of the table. It included a chit signed in her own hand.

She suppressed a glower, for she would not be dubbed bitter in defeat. It was evident from his immaculate dress—a perfectly tied cravat, a waistcoat sewn from the finest silk and a coat cut to fit his broad shoulders in tight embrace—that Rockwell had not her situation and was not in dire need of funds. She watched him replace a beautiful onyx ring upon his hand and found herself regarding his rugged fingers. She had never before paid much heed to a man's hand—or a woman's for that matter—but his conveyed strength, agility and even gentleness.

Dismissing the odd warmth that flared in her of a sudden, she glanced about the gaming hell for someone she might harry to lend her fifty quid. But the hour was late, the patrons at her table had left half an hour ago, and many of those remaining had debts themselves to pay. If only she had quit while ahead, but she had derived too much satisfaction from besting a man who possessed all that she did not—wealth, refined features and a quiet assurance that bordered on arrogance.

"I will repay you from my next winnings," she informed Rockwell.

"I have a better repayment option for you, Miss Herwood."

She raised her brows and waited patiently as he returned his purse to his coat. He looked across the card table at her. His dark-brown eyes reflected either the light of the candelabras or some inner merriment. His stare unsettled her, but not as much as what he said next.

"I would have you in my bed, Miss Herwood. For one night, I will take my pleasure of you, after which, your debt to me will be acquitted in its entirety."

"You would make of me a whore?" she asked when she had collected her wits and realized that he did not speak in jest. No one would mistake her family for members of the *ton*, but neither did her status merit such an affront.

"Let us have no pretentions, Miss Herwood. You relinquished your maidenhead years ago."

Her cheeks—nay, her entire countenance—flushed to know that he was privy to such confidence. Younger and more impulsive, she had surrendered her maidenhead to a man she thought would care for her. A colonel in His Majesty's Army, he was called to service before their affair could blossom into anything of consequence. Having lost her honor, she saw no reason subsequently not to indulge in the occasional affair, but she had always proceeded with great discretion. Her family had already suffered a fall from grace when she became a regular at the gaming hell, and she would not worsen the situation with more scandal.

Holding his gaze, she replied, "You overestimate the appeal of your company, Lord Rockwell. I would sooner double my obligation."

"Suit yourself," he said with dispassion and rose to his feet.

She considered how many hands of *vingt-et-un* she would have to win to secure fifty pounds and the litany of woes she would hear from her mother and aunt should she fail to bring home any income. They were a household of women since her father passed away, and the want of a man was never more palpable than now. If she could erase a debt of fifty pounds through one act—one night—might she be a fool to pass upon such an opportunity? As Lord Rockwell's barefaced assertion indicated, she no longer had any claim to a maiden's honor.

But what did she know of the man? Very little. He was not a frequent patron of her gaming hell. They had perhaps shared a card table once before; he had not taken much notice of her then. She, however, had not overlooked his presence, nor the women who threw themselves his way.

He possessed a countenance she would have

enjoyed studying at length, much in the way one would admire a painting or sculpture. If he favored a lass here or there, it was difficult to ascertain, though surely no mortal could resist such attentions for long. Years ago, she had heard that banns would be read betwixt him and a Spanish princess or the daughter of a Duke or some such. Admittedly, the lack of a wedding ring was one of the first things she had noted when he sat down at her table this evening.

That he was always impeccably dressed also did not escape her, but many a man spent money he did not possess in order to maintain the appearance of wealth. She would not have allowed the wager to reach the sum of fifty pounds had she not felt assured of Lord Rockwell's finances. Unlike others, he did not flaunt his affluence. And though down by an even grander sum at one point, he showed no apprehension at the loss. How quickly thereafter the game had betrayed her!

Regardless of what she knew or thought of the man, her situation remained. If she did not accept his proposition, she was indebted to him for a significant amount of money. His demeanor suggested if she rebuffed him tonight, he would not necessarily renew his proposal.

"Pray, wait."

Lord Rockwell paused and looked down at her.

"I accept your offer," she informed him with eyes downcast. Honor or no, she could not look at him.

He inclined his head. "You honor me, Miss Herwood."

What a ridiculous statement, she thought, as if she had accepted an invitation for a ride in the park with him.

"There are rooms here reserved for more, er, amorous pursuits. Shall we retire to one of them?" she inquired, meeting his gaze this time, then wishing she hadn't. The contrast of dark intensity with the glimmer of light in his eyes disconcerted her.

"That won't do. The accommodations here are hardly adequate," he replied. "My carriage shall meet you here two nights hence. The wait will deepen the anticipation."

*Anticipation? His or hers?* Perhaps his self-assurance was arrogance after all.

"My only request," he continued with a stern tone, "is that you do not arrive inebriated."

Again, she reddened. She was known to have had a glass too many on occasion, but how did this man whom she barely knew acquire such knowledge of her? And why should it matter to him what state she was in? Lest he was expecting her to perform certain acts upon him? The thought made her blush deeper.

His features softened as he lifted her hand to his lips. "*Au revoir.*"

As she watched him depart, she began to regret her decision, for she could not attribute to indignation alone the warmth she felt spreading throughout her.

\* \* \* \* \*

"Are you headed to that gaming hell again?" her aunt queried as Deana finished her supper and prepared to leave the table. "You'll never find a husband if you waste your hours there in the company of cads and rogues."

"Leave her be," her mother responded. "We can ill afford her not to go. It were not as if she had any marital prospects to entertain."

On that merry note, Deana ascended the stairs to her bedroom. Had she known her father would pass from an untimely failure of the heart, she would have sought matrimony earlier. While he had earned a decent income as a barrister, they had over time eaten into what savings they had, including funds intended as her dowry. If it were not for a flair and more luck than not at the card tables, she knew not how they would have fared. She had to acquit herself of her debt to Lord Rockwell or her hours at the gambling hall would be long indeed.

Struggling with her attire, she settled first on her plainest muslin, but vanity, and perhaps a subtle desire to please Lord Rockwell, led her to a simple but elegant gown of batiste. She could not deny a part of her was flattered that he wished to bed her. He had a physiognomy pleasing to the eye, a physique that knew few rivals, and a grace to his movements and carriage. She had relived the kiss to her hand over and over despite herself. The firmness, the gentleness with which he had held her hand and the deliberateness in how he had released her made her quiver. Though not uncomely herself, she would be as naïve as a schoolroom chit to think she was a skirt of singular interest to him. There were rumors enough of the women he had taken to bed, and undoubtedly others that had not risen to the level of tittle-tattle.

At the gaming hell, she drummed her fingers against the card table before bolstering her courage with a third glass of burgundy. She played a few rounds of faro, hoping that in the final minutes Lady Luck would spare her the humiliation of prostituting herself for a mislaid wager. She had assumed Lord Rockwell to be discreet, for she had not known him to confirm any of his *liaisons*, but she had no guarantee of his confidence. Granted, her patronage of a gaming hell had already diminished her repute, but word of her lifting her skirts to Lord Rockwell would discharge any prospects for matrimony—the only stable salvation for her family.

"Your carriage awaits, Miss Herwood," a footman informed her.

She retrieved her gloves and hat, pulling its veil low over her face before she stepped into the carriage. By the time it pulled up in front of Lord Rockwell's Town home, the burgundy had calmed her anxiety and put her in a more cheerful disposition. She had consumed three glasses of wine in the past with no significant impacts. Despite his command that she arrive sober, he would be no wiser. No doubt he differed little from others of his sex and, after twenty minutes, she would find him spent, her obligation complete, and herself returned home before midnight.

Once inside, the butler offered to take her pelisse but she declined. He showed her into the drawing room. Compared to her address, the room was richly furnished and its décor stately but not garish. The gleam of the wood and the shine of the upholstery indicated the furnishings to be new or well cared for, unlike the few pieces her family owned or borrowed. A healthy fire kept the room warm and the candelabras on the silken walls gave it light. A small elephant carved from ivory caught her eye. She picked it up from the end table and admired the detailing and its two ruby eyes.

"Do sit, Miss Herwood."

She bobbled the figurine before clutching it tightly to her chest to keep it from falling. She turned in the direction of the rich tenor.

Lord Rockwell stood at the threshold, appearing as dapper in his banyan as he did in full dress. Quickly she returned the elephant to its home. The thought that she had nearly dropped what was no doubt an expensive item made her tremble. God knew what she would owe him then.

"Two and twenty thousand rupees," he answered. "It belonged to a Hindu rajah."

"It's beautiful," she murmured.

"Sit, Miss Herwood."

His imperial tone contrasted with the more courteous manners he exhibited at the gaming hell. Perhaps he fancied himself a rajah in his own abode. Though tempted to defy him, she sat down upon a settee, noting that tea had been set upon the table before it. He sat opposite her and poured her a cup, which she accepted gratefully, for she would not know what to do with her hands otherwise. She took a sip of the fragrant Darjeeling, ignoring his penetrating gaze.

"You're inebriated," he stated with a frown.

*Damn. How the bloody hell did he discern that?* Caught, she opted to mask her embarrassment with childish insolence.

"I had myself a glass," she admitted with a dismissive shrug, avoiding his stare by focusing on her tea. "I am no child, Lord Rockwell, and you are not my guardian."

"Indeed. If I were, you would certainly not be spending your time in a gaming hell."

"And if I were yours, you would not be making indecent propositions to ladies you hardly know."

His brows rose but his eyes glimmered with amusement.

"Such insolence can be tamed," he said almost to himself, then offered her the plate of biscuits. "You will require sustenance to soak up the effects of the wine."

She hesitated. The wine was giving her courage, but perhaps it was best she had all her wits about her with this man.

"The servants have all retired for the evening. You've no need to conceal yourself."

"You will forgive me if I fail to trust to assurances alone that our transaction, if you will, shall remain private."

After a moment of thought, he went to the writing table and retrieved paper and pen. After a quick scrawl, he affixed his seal and handed her the note.

"You may redeem this if the confidence of this night is broken," he told her.

She choked on her tea upon seeing the amount he had penned. Five hundred pounds!

"Do you make such offers to all the women you take to bed?" she could not help asking.

His expression darkened and she regretted her impudence.

"Consider yourself unique, Miss Herwood."

There was a peculiar strain to his voice. She took another sip of the tea to avoid his gaze. Of course the other women willingly lifted their skirts to him. She wondered if she would have done the same had she not lost to him.

"When do we, er, begin…?"

"Our 'transaction'?"

"Would you prefer a more romantic term?" she replied archly.

"Not at all. I have always observed you to be practical and devoid of the silly sensibilities and nonsense that permeate others of your sex."

He had observed her before? Should she be flattered by this? She began to wonder if he had deliberately chosen to sit at her card table the other night.

"We will conduct our matter when you are in full possession of your faculties," he continued, pouring her more tea, "that you may fully appreciate its aspects."

She could not help an unladylike snort. "You fancy yourself an accomplished lover, do you?"

He said nothing, but a smile tugged at the corner of his lips. They were a sensuous pair. For a moment, she wondered what it would feel like to be kissed by them. She shook herself back to attention, glad the veil shielded her, to a degree, from his discerning stare. The wine was having the damnable effect of making the man more attractive.

"I think you will find the experience agreeable, Miss Herwood."

"And how do you come to merit such arrogance?"

"You will discover for yourself soon enough."

She pursed her lips in frustration. She had hoped for a short visit and instead of concluding their business, they were having a *tête-à-tête* over bloody tea. Setting aside her cup, she untied her pelisse and allowed it to fall from her shoulders.

"Did you not wish to take your pleasure of me?"

A muscle along his jaw rippled as he settled further into the settee. "In due time."

*Tiresome man.*

Those with wealth and countenance assumed the world revolved about them. A rush of envy stoked a darker side of her. In the end he was but a man, with base desires no different than a commoner, and she would prove it so. She unpinned her hat and fixed her most smoldering stare upon him. She had witnessed the coquetry of the women who patronized the gaming hell and been entertained by how simply a man could be lured into their grasps.

"Have you ever considered becoming a courtesan to relieve your fiscal conditions?"

His uncanny ability to know her thoughts unnerved her, and the truth of the matter struck a vulnerable chord. She had considered the option but simply had no prospects at the moment.

"If you are offering, Lord Rockwell, I am flattered but must decline," she retorted as she removed her gloves, slowly peeling one past her elbow and exposing the smooth, pale skin of her forearm.

The corner of his mouth quirked upward. They both knew he had no intention of inviting her to be his mistress, but her response amused him. His gaze fell to her bare arms. The heat in his eyes made her feel as if she had taken off all her garments, not just her gloves. Emboldened by his appreciation, she angled herself on the settee and put a hand to the nape of her neck.

"I seem to have missed a pin," she said. "Would my lord oblige in removing it?"

He made no movement, making her wonder whether her inexperience in playing the coquette appeared that obvious, but then he crossed the distance between them and sat down beside her, his thigh dangerously close to her rump. She felt his fingers upon her hair and suppressed a shiver.

"You are mistaken, Miss Herwood. I see none."

She could sense the warmth of his body, and when he trailed a knuckle down the length of her neck, she suddenly wanted him to grab her and kiss her. But he had resumed his seat opposite her, leaving her wanting. She frowned. *He* had propositioned *her*. Did he expect that *she* would throw herself at *him*? Looking into his eyes, she suspected that he knew the effect he had on her. But she must have impressed him to some degree or he would not have offered to forfeit fifty pounds for one night of attention. Granted, fifty pounds was no significant sum for him, but he could have had women of far more consequence at his beck and call for far less.

Inspired by this reasoning, she stood up and sauntered toward him.

"Shall we retire to your bedchamber, my lord?"

"I prefer different quarters."

His response struck her as odd, but the sofa upon which he sat appeared comfortable enough. She dropped to her knees, the wine humming in her veins. Surprise lighted his eyes but he did not move. His gaze caressed the swell of her cheek, the skin above her décolletage and, seeming to penetrate the material of her dress, the curves beneath. Her body tingled from head to toe beneath his regard. She dared to put a hand upon his knee. When he did not flinch, she glanced into his countenance and thought she saw flames in his eyes.

"You have managed to learn the arts of a courtesan," he observed coolly, with only the faintest hitch in his voice.

Her heart hammered in her ears. She was a novice playing with fire. Never before had she been so bold with a man. But never before had she dealt with a man who refused to be seduced by the very woman he had propositioned.

"You have finished neither your biscuit nor your tea, Miss Herwood."

"I have no need for your tea and biscuit. I am in full command of my faculties, Lord Rockwell, despite the presence of a bit of wine," she responded.

"Ah, Miss Herwood, how poorly you lie."

She would have risen, thrown her hands up in exasperation and reached for her gloves and hat, daring him to stop her from leaving, but he had cupped her chin in one hand, his forefinger lazily grazing the soft spot beneath her jaw. She fought the desire to melt into his hand and the weakening in her limbs, for she had to uphold her earlier assertion. It was no easy battle, and the wine, which had hitherto been her supporter, turned foe in this matter.

"You contravened my command. I would have overlooked one glass of wine, but you have partaken of more, Miss Herwood."

Command? The word jolted her to attention and she pulled away from him. His touch rattled her senses far too much.

"You insist upon playing my guardian, Lord Rockewell?"

He smiled. "If that were the case, you would be splayed across my lap for a sound spanking."

Her mouth went dry at the thought. A small voice inside advised her to run from this man. At the very least she ought to put some distance between them, but a darker side of her was drawn to him more than ever.

"Patience, my dear Miss Herwood," he gently coaxed.

Patience? Would he have her return to her seat, twiddle with the damn biscuits and wait...wait for what?

"Have I misunderstood your proposition, Lord Rockwell? Did you not say that I could discharge my debt if I were to lay with you?"

"I did proffer one night of pleasure."

"And by pleasure you meant a *tête-à-tête* over tea? La! How silly of me to have suspected you of more roguish intentions."

As she spoke, she realized a part of her would be quite disappointed if he answered in the affirmative. She rose to her feet but he grabbed her at the wrist and pulled her across him with startling deftness. How easily he manhandled her.

"Make no mistake, Miss Herwood. I intend to take my pleasure of you," he growled, his mouth beside her ear.

"Then why delay, my lord?" she whispered back against his ear over the loud thumping of her heart.

He made a low groan. Before she could react, he had pinned her against the arm of the sofa. His mouth was atop hers, crushing, claiming, punishing. She had never been kissed with such force and felt a surge of triumph. Her head swam from the heady combination of intoxication and arousal. She attempted to return his forceful kiss, but his mouth dictated the terms. He tasted of her, explored her, consumed her. She could do little but surrender to his attentions.

When at last he released her to breathe, and the world had slowed its swirl about her head, she could not resist saying, "Patience, my lord."

"Patience be damned," he returned, though the glint in his eye had her suspecting that perhaps her triumph was not as complete as she would think

# CHAPTER TWO

She did not dwell long for he captured her mouth once more in his and she was content to revel in his desire for her. He trailed his lips down her neck and her back arched of its own volition, pressing her body into his, feeling the weight of him. She had not expected that area to prove so sensitive. As if cognizant of that delicacy, he kissed her with feathery lightness, a contrast to the vehemence with which he had plumbed her mouth earlier. His hand went to the small of her back, and that too proved provocative. She felt surrounded by him.

Desire swelled below her waist. She put her hand to the back of his neck, brushing the ends of his hair as he nestled into her neck. Forgetting her intentions to make quick her obligation to him, she allowed him to take his time caressing her décolletage and skimming the tops of her breasts. She had expected him to ravish them. In her previous encounters, the men had torn at her bodice as if they were starving babes eager to nurse, but she sensed that Lord Rockwell was no callow lover. Her nipples hardened, desiring his attention. As if sensing her precise need, he cupped a breast and grazed the nipple with his thumb. Her breath caught as a jolt of sensation shot from her nipple to the apex of her thighs. His thumb circled the nipple, rubbing the fabric of her dress into the bud until she squirmed and moaned her need for release.

He slid his hand to her upper thigh. Would he now throw up her skirts and mount her? She found she did not dread the prospect. Indeed, the carnal yearning within her welcomed it. But instead of unbuttoning his trousers, he pulled up the hem of her dress and ran his hand along her leg. How she wished she had a better pair of stockings to present to a man who undoubtedly knew all the luxuries in life. He brushed the soft skin just above the stockings with his knuckles, his hand dangerously close to where her desire pooled hot and wet.

She glanced into his face. His soft brown eyes gleamed in a manner that made her reconsider once more the wisdom of her intoxication. He had the upper hand in more ways than one. But she had no time to chide herself for his fingers skimmed the patch of hair at the base of her pelvis. His thumb slipped lower and teased that small but potent nub of flesh between her legs. She closed her eyes against his stare, marveling at the delicious disconcertion in her body. Lightly he fondled her clitoris, nipped it between two fingers, stroked its length 'til she was panting. Her body, now a coil that needed unwinding , strained to his touch. In response he deepened his caress. Dipping a finger into her hot wetness, he rubbed her with increasing vigor.

Gasping, she felt herself thrown over a familiar

precipice, only it felt more glorious than when she attended to her needs in solitude. She erupted in uncontrolled paroxysms against him. A cry escaped her lips. He pushed the last of the spasms from her body before easing his caress into a gentle swirling. She shuddered.

"You spend beautifully, Miss Herwood."

She barely heard his words. Lost in a fog of relief and glory and the remnants of her inebriation, she allowed herself to sink into the sofa. If he wanted her to attend him, he would have to wait and acquire some of the patience he had advocated earlier.

\* \* \* \* \*

Deana fluttered her eyes. Settled in a haze of comfort and satisfaction, she had no desire to move, but the aroma of fresh coffee called to her. She glanced down at the luxurious blanket covering her legs and felt the firm cushions beneath her. Her gaze moved to the porcelain coffee set in front of her and then across the table to the opposite sofa where Lord Rockwell sat, one leg crossed over the other, his expression soft.

Good heavens, had she fallen asleep?

Quickly she sat up, but the speed of her motions made the side of her head throb.

"Coffee will aid your situation," he offered, pouring a cup.

Flushing, she took the hot beverage with gratitude. He was correct—she should not have come intoxicated. She noticed he was no longer wearing his banyan or any neckwear. Instead, the top buttons of his shirt were undone—a minor feature but grandly provocative. Memories of what had transpired betwixt them rushed into her mind, warming her body instantly.

"Forgive my impoliteness for having, er, fallen asleep on your settee," she said more to her coffee than to him. She had never fallen asleep in a strange place before.

"I am glad for it," he replied. "Do you drink often, Miss Herwood?"

She eyed him carefully. "You seem to know much about me. Do you not already have your answer, your lordship?"

"A gaming hell is no place for one of the fair sex to let down her guard."

"I am no fool nor child."

"Tonight being the exception?"

She tried not to glare at him. "Though I am sure you are accustomed to women throwing themselves at you, might you allow that one would deem the situation I find myself facing rather daunting?"

His lips curved in genuine humor and she found it hard to remain angry with him. How glorious those lips had felt upon her…

"Miss Herwood?"

Realizing she had been staring at his mouth, she buried her face in her coffee. What a gauche young woman he must perceive her to be!

"Please partake of the sweatmeats." He gestured to the berries, cheese and bread on the coffee tray.

Though not particularly hungry, she decided to eat as a distraction and idly wondered if he had woken the servants in the middle of the night to prepare the coffee.

He poured himself a cup and settled back into the sofa to gaze upon her. She wanted to quip about the impoliteness of staring, but the entitled would not care for comments from one such as her. Instead, she broke the silence with small talk.

"Do you travel to India often?"

"What do you consider often? It is no easy journey."

She had no definition in mind. The farthest she had ever been from London was Bath.

"Would you venture there if it were not?" she rephrased.

He weighed her query. "In truth, I am ambivalent. There is much to wonder at and detest of the East."

She tried to fathom a world she had seen only in books and an occasional painting, but in her mind danced colorful silks, teas and curries.

"Tell me of India."

"Many would find her easy to disdain, but you would appreciate India."

"You know me well enough to make such a declaration?"

"I merely observe the inflection when you speak and the shine in your eyes. You are not difficult to read, Miss Herwood."

She frowned. She was gauche *and* guileless?

"Do not distress yourself. Consider it a compliment. I find it refreshing."

Is that what had attracted him to her table?

"I imagine a visitor from India could find much to disdain in England," she remarked. "For instance, certain noblemen can be quite insufferable here."

He grinned at her taunt. "I couldn't agree more, Miss Herwood. More coffee?"

She eagerly accepted, for the coffee did aid with her headache and she was beginning to enjoy her conversation with Lord Rockwell.

"I think you are partial to India, Lord Rockwell."

"Indeed?"

She gestured about the room. "You have reminders of her everywhere."

He followed her gaze from the elephant she had held earlier to a bronze oil lamp above the fireplace to a tapestry on the wall. The image on the tapestry was a woman wearing a golden headdress, arms stretched with a bow and arrow, astride a many-hued parrot.

"Rati," he explained. "Hindu goddess of love, passion and carnal pleasure."

Her cheeks colored. She recalled her purpose for being here and, as she had pointed out earlier, it was not for conversation.

"How appropriate," she murmured. "I am aware that I have not fulfilled my end of the arrangement, my lord."

"Not entirely. I took great pleasure in seeing you spend."

Her whole body flushed. She shifted under his gaze.

The fires in his eyes flared. "I have much more planned, Miss Herwood."

She swallowed with difficulty the coffee she had just imbibed and felt a strong need to fan herself.

"How do you wish to begin?" she croaked.

"Come here," he said, his tone gentle and commanding.

She went to stand before his sofa. He rose to his feet. Looking down at her, he brushed a stray tendril of hair over her shoulder.

"What does your body desire most, Miss Herwood?" he asked.

*You.* At that moment, she realized that she had never desired a man as much as she did then. The embers from his recent caresses were quick to burn anew.

"My lord?"

"What brings you the greatest pleasure?" He slid the back of his forefinger down her neck and along her collarbone.

"Having a romp at the tables against haughty noblemen."

He circled his arm around her waist and jerked her to him. She could feel his hardened arousal against her hip.

"I promise you will enjoy having lost to me, Miss Herwood." As he held her against him, his other hand cupped her jaw and lifted her face. "You shall not soon forget this night."

"And what have I done to merit such a prospect?" she asked quietly, momentarily mesmerized by the depths of his eyes. Like diamonds, they reflected an inner fire.

His thumb passed over her mouth, tugging the bottom lip down. He grazed the tip of her tongue. She caught his thumb in her mouth and sucked. Hard.

He groaned. Removing his thumb, he replaced it with his mouth. She could taste the coffee and, beyond that, him. His mouth covered hers, his tongue probed and coaxed. Her head was spinning, she had never experienced such a full and luscious kiss. Deeper he went but in steps that assured she could follow. Not at all like her last lover, who harkened to her mind a pet dog she once had. The dear little bitch would greet her with all tongue, lapping at her face and drowning her in slaver.

Lord Rockwell's kiss was consuming but purposeful. His lips led hers in a heady dance that left her breathless and wanting. His cock felt like a steel rod against her. She pressed her hips to him, the carnal yearning in her body needing to connect with his. He responded by gripping her tighter, one hand cupping a buttock so that she remained molded to him. She let out a small gasp. He dropped his head and tongued the hollow of her neck. Any lingering regrets of having lost to Lord Rockwell at the card table vanished. She wanted him to take her and satiate the burning within her. Wrapping her arms around his neck, she pulled him into her. She would be content to kiss for an eternity but for the ache building within her. Her hand slid from his neck to the slight opening of his shirt.

Abruptly he whipped her around and pinned her backside against him. The thickness of his desire pressed against her derriere. One arm circled her chest, the other her pelvis. She could have melted into his embrace. As he rained kisses along her neck, he groped a breast, kneading the flesh through her dress. Her nipple puckered beneath his touch. She wanted his other hand to pull up her skirts as he had done and fondle once more that most sensitive of parts.

Taking her by the hand, he led across the drawing room and, pulling a key from his pocket, unlocked a door she had not noticed before.

The room she entered was dark but for two bronze oil lamps on either side of a grand four-post bed of mahaony with a blood-red canopy and golden tassles and orange silk curtains, large plush pillows, and silk bedclothes. It was beautiful, fit for an Indian princess. "How lovely," she mururmed.

"It pleases you?"

"I supposed it were as fine a setting as any for the…" she began.

He had cme up behind her. She tensed. His presence alone could send her judgment scattering. Already her body responded as if being called by sirens.

"The transaction," he supplied, "or let us call it what it is: a night of debauchery, of the finest pleasures."

She closed her eyes at his seductive voice but resisted.

"Finest pleasures? I hope your words signify you will not be too difficult to please."

"I was referring to *your* pleasure."

"Mine? You are bold, my lord."

"Have I not attended you with satisfaction?"

He ran a finger up her bare arm and she could not quell a shiver. How had her body become so sensitized to his touch?

"What you require is beyond the norm," she murmured.

He rested his hand upon her shoulder, then gently began rubbing away the tension.

"I would not have invited you here if I did not think you possessed a bold spirit. I shall do nothing you cannot bear. All that I do is for your desire."

She raised a brow. "You presume to know my desires?"

The corner of his mouth curled upward. "And they shall be provided a most rapturous end."

She shook her head. "Your presumption knows no bounds."

His eyes glimmered. "Care to lay wager upon it, Miss Herwood?"

"Despite my conviction, I think I had best not."

"Then to allay your fears, allow me to propose that if you do not find this night to be fulfilling, I will offer as recompense the sum of one hundred pounds."

A hundred quid! She salivated at the sum. She could stall the creditors from repossessing the furniture. Her mother could indulge in jam and butter upon her toast.

"And how would you define fulfillment?"

He trailed his hand down to the swell of her breast. "Not I. You shall—with your orgasm. The absence of it would mark a night unfulfilled."

She gazed down at his hand. One hundred pounds. And she had but to refrain from spending?

"You mock me, Lord Rockwell."

"I rarely jest on such matters."

His hand dipped beneath her décolletage and cradled a breast. She closed her eyes. His touch was exquisite.

"Do you make a habit of such outrageous propositions?"

"Would you believe me if I said I did not?"

"No."

He kissed her lightly upon the neck. "Then why

ask?"

She sighed. Exasperating if not clever man.

He whipped her around and pressed his mouth full upon hers.

"Come, I dare you to accept the wager," he murmured against her lips.

# CHAPTER THREE

The warmth between her legs flared once more, but she forced her mind to the task. "You have me at a disadvantage. I have but your word that you will honor both the word of safety and your wager."

He pulled back and stared deep into her eyes. "Your dilemma is understandable. I can only ask that you trust me."

Her heart throbbed with excitement and fear. Thriving in a gaming hell necessitated the constant assessment of character, and her instincts gave no alarm with Lord Rockwell. She wanted to place herself in his hands, but she barely knew the man. And yet she had never felt more at ease in a man's company.

A hundred pounds. It was too grand a sum not to take the risk.

"Very well, Lord Rockwell, I accept."

His smile reached his eyes and she sensed her relief reflected also in him.

"I promise you will not rue the hand you lost at

*vingt-et-un.*"

He led her to a mirror and stood once more behind her. It was most disconcerting for she knew not what he would do, nor could she read his countenance.

"Tell me what arouses you," he instructed as his hand brushed the skin above the back of her bodice.

"You are most forward, Lord Rockwell, and I have no intention of giving you any assistance in winning your wager."

She saw his smile in the mirror.

"Touché. I will discern the answer nonetheless."

He began to unbutton her gown.

Dialogue could prove a good distraction, she decided. "How many women have you entertained in this chamber of yours?"

The answer should dampen her lust.

"You are most forward, Miss Herwood."

She could not help a grin at his response.

"I have not kept count."

"Several?"

"Define 'several'."

He eased the top of her gown down her arms. It pooled at her feet. She watched in the mirror as he untied her petticoats next.

"Four or more?"

"Or more, certainly."

The petticoats fell to the ground. She blushed at the sight of herself in stays and shift. He began to unlace her stays without effort.

"Should not a man of your stature be seeking a wife instead of indulging in prurient interests?" she asked, averting her eyes from the mirror.

"Should not a woman of your situation be seeking a

husband instead of gambling at a gaming hell?" he returned.

She bristled. "I asked first."

"A wife is easy enough to attain. I see no reason to rush."

How she wished she could claim the same of a husband!

"I am earning my dowry, if you will, at the gaming hell."

Clever response, she praised herself.

"You require a husband with funds, not a man in search of a dowry."

She pursed her lips at his obvious statement, which made quick work of her smugness.

"It is no easy matter to find a man with funds and possessing a decent character."

"Especially in a gaming hell."

Their dialogue was proving quite effective, for now anger trumped all that she felt. To her surprise, tears threatened. She was well aware that her current finances necessitated her spending time in a gaming hell, which dimmed her marital prospects and future security.

"You see the irony of my situation then," she replied with an edge. "I have not the fortune to have been born into the *ton* or with a bounty of assets at my disposal."

The stays dropped from her.

"I beg to differ," Rockwell said.

She saw herself wearing only her chemise, stockings and garters.

He slid the sleeve of the shift down a shoulder and kissed her there. "You have remarkable assets."

He gripped the flimsy fabric and tore it in twain down the front, exposing her breasts, her abdomen, her pelvis. She gasped and stared at the mirror in shock. Modesty finally set in and she looked away. As if his words had not riled her enough, he had to destroy her shift as well?

"I will compensate you for your loss, but look in the mirror, Deana."

She should chastise him for the familiar use of her name, but she fixed her concentration upon the ground.

"Look," he ordered in a tone she found difficult to disobey.

She moved her gaze to the mirror.

"You are lovely."

He pulled the torn garment from her and circled his arms around to cup her breasts.

"In addition to many other fine attributes in your possession," he continued.

He tugged at her nipples and all her anger dissipated, replaced with a poignant need. She looked away once more, but he took her chin and directed her to the mirror.

"Look at yourself," he commanded.

She raised her eyes.

"I am no poet," he said, "or I could speak eloquently of these."

Once more he fondled her breasts. Desire warmed in her loins despite the awkwardness of having to look upon her own nakedness.

"And these."

His hands dropped to her hips.

"And this."

One hand reached the triangle of hair at her groin. How delicious his warm, strong hands felt upon her body…

*A hundred pounds*, she reminded herself.

"You have the body of a goddess."

His voice was a caress as powerful as his touch.

"That of lithe Artemis," he continued, "or Athena."

He took both her hands in his and guided them to her breasts and over her belly. He moved their right hands between her thighs. She gasped. She was touching herself in front of him! He stroked her flesh through her fingers. His left hand moved hers back to a breast, palming the mound, rolling it over her chest. She needed to escape the assault of sensations but tried not to squirm. He began strumming against her flesh, bumping her fingers into herself. She squeezed her thighs together to limit the movements but he managed to push her forefinger into her wet, hot cunnie.

*Dear God, he's making me frig myself.* She was both aroused and flustered. He lifted his head to see her countenance. The flash in his eyes made her heart thump even more. He pushed her finger deeper inside her while he pressed his thumb upon her clit. Gradually he increased the motions of both hands. Her head fell against his shoulder at the onslaught. She could look no more. Wonderful sensations brewed and ricocheted inside her.

*A hundred pounds. A hundred pounds. A hundred pounds.*

"Do not move," he said, withdrawing his hands.

She saw herself in the mirror, one hand upon her breast, the other buried between her legs. Her flesh throbbed about her finger. When he stepped away to retrieve something, she pulled out of herself and covered herself.

"You moved," he scolded upon his return.

The darkness of his tone quickened her pulse. A threat lay beneath his words. She saw he held a length of rope. What was *that* for?

"And I have yet to punish you, Miss Herwood, for your first indiscretion."

She could barely speak but managed to croak, "My lord?"

"I specifically told you not to come inebriated."

She felt like a chastened child but retorted, "I forget you are accustomed to women doing all that you bid."

He pulled the rope taut between his hands and sauntered over to the bed. "By all means, contravene me at every turn. I shall have as little qualm in administering punishment as I do pleasure. Come here."

After some hesitation, she complied, praying that she would not regret her decision to place all trust in him. With the servants asleep, there would be no one to come to her rescue should she need it. She doubted they would hear her screams through the door and down into the servants' quarters.

He positioned her before one of the bedposts and, pulling her arms up, tied her wrists above her to the post. Her heart beat rapidly. Did he intend her harm? Her intuition had never suggested the possibility to her, but why would he bind her to the bed?

"Is this necessary?" she asked, testing the bonds to see if she could escape if needed. They held fast.

"I find the placement of one's hands to be an unnecessary distraction," he replied, stepping back to look her over. "You may attend your enjoyment better this way."

He cradled a breast, then kneaded the flesh. He passed a thumb over the nipple, causing it to harden further. She shivered.

"And it permits me complete freedom to have my way with you," he finished.

She was about to protest the necessity of being tied to the bed when his mouth covered her nipple, dashing all words from her. The wet warmth encasing the sensitive bud sent her senses reeling. He sucked, taking her breath as well and sending flutters from her bosom to her loins. For several minutes he toyed with the nipple—licking, tugging, nipping. Closing her eyes, she tried not to let the sensations overhwlem her. She squirmed against the bedpost and was now partially glad that he had bound her hands for she knew not whether she wanted to push him away or pull him closer.

When he stopped, she opened her eyes to find him assessing her. Her gaze caught in his, she sensed she could have been prey he intended to devour. His mouth descended upon hers. She could do nothing but submit to his ferocious kiss and understood then why he had wanted her sober—that she could appreciate every maddening sensation. When he released her from his kiss, she felt as if a fine wine had been dashed from her lips. She wanted more, wanted his tongue to continue probing her depths.

But a hundred pounds was at stake, she reminded herself and did her best to quell her nerves.

"You are quite delectable, Miss Herwood," he murmured as a hand slipped between her legs to her wetness. She groaned. He teased and tormented that traitorous nub of desire there. Despite her efforts to resist, she felt the arousal intensifying, felt herself growing hotter and wetter. She shifted, against both the constraints of the rope and the ache emanating from within.

With his free hand, he attended her other breast, groping her, pinching the nipple. Her breath grew erratic as she writhed beneath his dual ministrations and the beautiful agony they created.

"Please," she mumbled after he had withdrawn his hands.

"Miss Herwood?"

Remembering their wager, she stopped herself from asking him to continue.

"Do you desire me to continue?" he inquired, his hand softly brushing the top of her thigh.

She could not think properly when he caressed her there, tantalizing close to where he had been touching her before. Of course she wanted him to continue— *not* to continue, that is.

His hand returned to the heat between her thighs. He strummed his fingers along her.

"Do you desire this?" he asked before slowing to a stop.

"Pray continue," she mumbled.

Silence.

Was he reveling in his victory? Glancing down, she saw the bulge at his crotch. Perhaps she was not the only one fighting back urges.

He resumed his stroking, stoking the tension in her

loins. Lubricated by her wetness, his hand created a delicious friction against her. She could not ignore the heat engulfing her body, the blood pumping in her veins. The odds of her winning the hundred quid were no longer in her favor. Her body craved to be led up to the precipice over which she would find release.

*Dear God.* Shutting her eyes, she tried to pretend the exquisiteness waving through her body were not hers. She was elsewhere. This woman at the mercy of Lord Rockwell, this woman bound and fondled was not her. *Think of something inane!*

Her mind went briefly to her aunts recounting their walks through Hyde Park, whom they saw, what was worn by those they saw, whom they didn't see…

She should not have asked him to continue! She cursed to herself. *A hundred pounds…*

As she warred with herself, he undid the rope. She had not realized how sore her arms were till they fell to her sides. Sweeping her into his arms, he carried her to the bed. He lay her on her stomach over a stack of pillows.

She heard the rustle of his clothes being shed and remembered how inviting his chest had looked beneath his shirt. Twisting her head, she looked behind herself to see his desire spring from his pants. Thick and hard, it was a beautiful member. She wanted it, needed it to tame the heat inside her.

*No, that will not do!* She needed to prevail with this wager. She forced her mind to consider the soreness in her arms and how unsettling it was to have her most intimate parts fully exposed and at his mercy.

And yet there was something quite titillating, exhilarating and seductive in submitting to Lord

Rockwell.

He encased his cock with a protective sheath. Partaking of her wetness, he rubbed it upon the covering and looked at her. The dark hunger in his eyes made her cunnie throb. She straightened her head and took a deep breath. When his erection grazed her, she gasped in delight. He sawed his erection between her legs. Back and forth. Back and forth. As pleasurable as the action was, she wanted more.

*Take me*, she nearly shouted.

As if reading her mind, he plunged himself into her. How marvelous he felt inside her. She would have savored the sensation longer but her arousal, brought to a famished height, was impatient for more. Her hips moved of their own volition. He moved his own in rhythm to hers until he was thrusting deeper and deeper into her. She moaned her appreciation. *Yes...*

*No.*

She managed to calm her hips. With her mind she tried to extinguish the fire consuming her. The effort made her feel as if her body would twist itself inside out.

He reached around her and pinched a nipple. The sensation shot straight to her quim. He continued his thrusting and circled his hand around her hip for her clitoris, stroking the engorged nub as he pumped in and out of her.

*No, no, no...yes...no...yes!*

Desire vibrated with unbearable intensity within her. The tide pushed against her now meager wall of resistance and her body shattered into a thousand pieces. She cried out as the waves washed over her.

Spasms rippled through her limbs, jerking her against him. She vaguely heard him grunt and felt his thrusts quicken before he fell atop her, his weight pushing her into the pillows. They lay, their bodies still joined, taking in air as they sank back to earth.

\* \* \* \* \*

A full sennight had passed since her visit with Lord Rockwell and still her cheeks flushed when she recalled their assignation. For days she could not sit without feeling the flogger upon her arse.

Applying a balm to the affected area, he had murmured, "Well done, Miss Herwood."

Despite having lost the wager, she had felt quite satisfied with herself. She had not required her safety word. Her body had been pushed to limits she had never thought possible. The whole experience had been *unworldly*.

With tenderness, he had removed her bonds and rubbed her sore arms as she lay against him, her body spent. And that too proved pleasurable. She would have been content to fall asleep in his arms but for the need to return before the household awoke. He had attended to her toilette with the air of a gentleman, notwithstanding what he had just done to her.

"I presume my debt to be disposed of?" she had inquired before departing.

His eyes had glimmered. "Indeed."

"Then I bid you good evening—or good day, rather."

"Good day, Miss Herwood."

He had lifted her hand to his lips. The kiss had sent

the embers of desire flaring and she would have been tempted to stay if he had asked her to.

"Oh that I could have a new ribbon for my bonnet. This one has lost its color and is more white than pink."

Her aunt's voice broke into her reverie.

Deana studied the petticoat she was mending for the fourth time. Perhaps she should have tried harder to win the hundred pounds from Lord Rockwell. She would not have minded another hand at cards with the man—and she was unsure whether she would prefer to win or lose against him.

She looked outside the drawing room window at the setting sun. It was almost the time when she would make her way to the gaming hell. The first few days she had looked for Rockwell often but he had not appeared. She could not help some disappointment at first. But why would a man like him seek her out again? He owed her nothing, not even a letter. They had said their farewell.

So she ought to turn her mind toward her customary pursuits and the constant goal of winning enough at cards to pay for the food upon their table. Her encounter with Lord Rockwell would be relegated to the past, an isolated exchange but one she would not look back upon without fondness.

"Dear, I hope it not be the creditors," her mother bemoaned.

Engrossed in her thoughts, Deana had not heard the knock at the door. She put down her sewing.

"I shall see to it."

She opened the door to a messenger holding a brown paper package.

"For Miss Herwood," the young man said.

Looking at her name upon the package, her heartbeat quickened. She recognized the hand. After thanking the boy, she quickly stole upstairs. In the privacy of her room, she carefully untied the string. She peeled back the wrapping and, lying in the middle of red and orange silks was a familiar ivory elephant with ruby eyes. Heart pounding, she picked it up gently. Beneath the elephant lay a simple note.

*For a most pleasurable evening.*

Smiling, she returned the elephant tenderly to the silk. A pleasurable evening indeed. Losing a hand at cards had never proved more delightful.

## THE END

# Georgette BROWN

# THAT WICKED HARLOT

EXCERPT FROM

# THAT
# WICKED
# HARLOT

# CHAPTER ONE

The beautiful woman wrapped in the arms of Radcliff M. Barrington, the fourth Baron Broadmoor, sighed into a wide smile as she nestled her body between his nakedness and the bed sheets. Gazing down at Lady Penelope Robbins, his mistress of nearly a twelvemonth, Broadmoor allowed her a moment to indulge in the afterglow of her third orgasm though he had yet to satisfy his own hardened arousal. He brushed his lips against her brow and happened to glance toward the corner of her bed chamber, where a man's waistcoat was draped over the back of a chair. He did not recognize it as his own. The fineness of the garment suggested that neither did it belong to one of her male servants.

Penelope was entertaining another lover, he concluded even as she murmured compliments regarding his skills as a lover. The realization came as no surprise to him. Indeed, he had suspected for some time. What surprised him was that he cared not overmuch. Nor had he the faintest curiosity as to who her other lover might be. He wondered, idly rather than seriously, why he continued to seek her company. Or she his. They had very little in common. He knew that from the start and yet had allowed her to seduce him into her bed.

He was possessed of enough breeding, wealth, and countenance to be able to command any number of women as his mistress. With black hair that waved above an ample brow and softened the square lines of his jaw, charcoal eyes that sparkled despite the dark hue, and an impeccable posture that made him taller than most of his peers, Broadmoor presented an impressive appearance. He had no shortage of women setting their caps at him. A number of his friends kept dancers or opera singers, but he had never been partial to breaking the hearts of those young things. In contrast, Penelope was a seasoned widow and had little expectation of him, having been married once before to a wealthy but vastly older baronet, and scorning a return to that institution, preferred instead to indulge in the freedoms of widowhood.

Pulling the sheets off her, he decided it was his turn to spend. She purred her approval when he covered her slender body with his muscular one. Angling his hips, he prepared to thrust himself into her when a shrill and familiar voice pierced his ears.

"I care not that he is indisposed! If the Baron is here, I *will* speak to him!"

The voice was imperial. Haughty. Broadmoor recognized it in an instant.

Penelope's eyes flew open. "Surely that is not your aunt I hear?"

His aunt, Lady Anne Barrington, was not wont to visit him in his own home at Grosvenor Square, let alone that of his mistress. He knew Anne found him cold, heartless, and arrogant. He had a dreadful habit of refusing to encourage her histrionics, and in the role of the indulgent nephew, he was a miserable failure.

"Let us pretend we do not hear her," Penelope added, wrapping her arms about him.

It would be easier to silence a skewered pig, Broadmoor thought to himself.

A timid but anxious knock sounded at the door.

"What is it?" Penelope snapped at the maid who entered and apologized profusely for the interruption, informing them that a most insistent woman waited in the drawing room and had threatened, if she was not attended to with the utmost haste, to take herself up the stairs in search of his lordship herself.

"I fear there is no immediate escape," Broadmoor said, kissing the frown on his mistress' brow before donning his shirt and pants and wrapping a robe about himself. "But I shall return."

Before descending the stairs, he took a moment for his arousal to settle.

*Whatever had compelled his aunt to come to the home of his mistress had better be of damned importance.*

"Anne. To what do I owe this unexpected visit?" he asked of his uncle's wife when he strode into the room.

He discerned Anne to be in quite a state of disconcertion for she only sported two long strands of pearls—far fewer than the five or so he was accustomed to seeing upon her. Her pale pink gown did not suit her complexion and made her pallor all the more grey in his eyes.

"Radcliff! Praise the heavens I have found you!" she cried upon seeing him.

He refrained from raising an inquisitive brow. Undaunted by the lack of response from her nephew, Anne continued, "We are *undone*, Radcliff! Undone! Ruined!"

His first thought was of her daughter, Juliana, who recently had had her come-out last Season. Had the girl run off to Gretna Green with some irascible young blood? He would not hesitate to give chase, but Juliana had always impressed him as a sensible young woman with an agreeable disposition—despite whom she had for a mother.

"I can scarce breathe with the thought!" Anne bemoaned. "And you know my nerves to be fragile! Oh, the treachery of it all!"

She began to pace the room while furiously waving the fan she clutched in her hand.

"I could never show my face after this," she continued. "How fortunate your uncle is not alive to bear witness to the most disgraceful ruin ever to befall a Barrington! Though I would that he had not left me to bear the burden all alone. The strain that has been put upon me—who else, I ask, has had to suffer not only the loss of her husband and now this—this unspeakable *disgrace*? I have no wish to speak ill of your uncle, but now I think it selfish of him to have gone off to the Continent with Wellington when he *knew* he would be put in harm's way. And for what end? What end?"

Broadmoor did not reveal his suspicions that his uncle had taken himself to the Continent as much as a means to relieve himself from being hen-pecked by his wife as for military glory. Instead, he walked over to the sideboard to pour her a glass of ratafia in the hopes that it would calm the incessant fluttering of her fan.

"And what is the nature of this ruin?" he prompted.

"The *worst imaginable!*" Anne emphasized in response to his complacent tenor. "Never in my life could I have conceived such misfortune! And to think we must suffer at *her* hands. That—that unspeakable wench. That *wicked harlot.*"

So it was the son and not the daughter, Broadmoor thought to himself. He should have expected it would be Edward, who was four years Juliana's senior but who possessed four fewer years to her maturity.

"You cannot conceive what torment I have endured these past days! And I have had no one, not a soul, to comfort me," Anne lamented, bypassing the ratafia as she worried the floor beneath her feet.

"The engagement to Miss Trindle has been called off?" Broadmoor guessed, slightly relieved for he did not think Edward up to the task of matrimony, even with the dowry of Miss Trindle serving as a handsome incentive. But it displeased him that Edward had not changed his ways.

"Heavens, no! Though it may well happen when the Trindles hear how we have been undone! Oh, but it is the fault of that devil-woman! My poor Edward, to have fallen victim to such a villainous lot."

Broadmoor suppressed a yawn.

"No greater ruin has *ever* befallen a Barrington," Anne added, sensing her nephew did not share her distress.

"Madam, my hostess awaits my attention," he

informed her, looking towards the stairs.

Anne burned red as she remembered where she was. "As this was a calamity—yes, a calamity—of the highest order, I could not wait. If your uncle were here, there would have been no need...well, perhaps. His disquiet could often worsen my state. But your presence, Radcliff, affords me hope. I have nowhere else to turn. And you were always quite sensible. I wish that you would learn Edward your ways. You were his trustee and have fifteen more years of wisdom than he. You might take him under your wing."

He raised an eyebrow at the suggestion. "Edward came of age last year when he turned twenty-one. He is master of his own fortune and free to ruin himself as he sees fit."

"How can you speak so?"

"I have intervened once already in Edward's life and have no wish to make a practice of it," Broadmoor replied coolly.

"But..."

He placed the ratafia in her hand before she sank into the nearest sofa, bereft of words in a rare moment for Anne Barrington.

"But that *darkie* is a hundred times worse than her sister!" Anne said upon rallying herself. "Oh, are we never to rid ourselves of this cursed family and their treachery?"

Broadmoor watched in dismay as she set down her glass and began agitating her fan before her as if it alone could save her from a fainting spell. He went to pour himself a glass of brandy, his hopes of a short visit waning.

"What will become of us?" Anne moaned. "What will become of Juliana? I had hopes that she would make a match this year! Did you know that the banns might be read for Miss Helen next month and she has not nearly the countenance that Juliana has!"

"What could Edward have done to place Juliana's matrimonial prospects in jeopardy?" he asked. "Juliana has breeding and beauty and one of the most desirable assets a young woman could have: an inheritance of fifty thousand pounds."

His aunt gave an indignant gasp. Her mouth opened to utter a retort or to comment on her nephew's insensitivity but thought better of it.

"But what are we to do without Brayten?" she asked with such despondency that Broadmoor almost felt sorry for her.

"I beg your pardon?"

"The thought overwhelms me. Indeed, I can scarcely speak, the nature of it is so dreadful..."

He refrained from pointing out the irony in her statement.

"Edward has lost Brayten."

It was Broadmoor's turn to be rendered speechless, but he quickly collected himself and said in a dark voice. "Lost Brayten? Are you sure of this?"

"When I think of the care and attention I lavished upon him—and to be repaid in such a fashion! To be undone in such a manner. And by that wretched harlot. What sort of odious person would prey upon an innocent boy like Edward?"

"Edward is far from innocent," he informed her wryly, "but how is it he could have lost Brayten?"

The boy was reckless, Broadmoor knew, but

Brayten was the sole source of income for Edward. The estate had been in the Barrington family for generations and boasted an impressive house in addition to its extensive lands. Surely the boy could not have been so careless as to jeopardize his livelihood.

"It is that witch, that hussy and devil-woman. They say she works magic with the cards. Witchcraft, I say!"

"Do you mean to tell me that Edward lost Brayten in a game of cards?" Broadmoor demanded.

"I had it from Mr. Thornsdale, who came to me at once after it had happened. I would that he had gone to you instead! Apparently, Edward had to wager Brayten to win back his obligation of eighty thousand pounds."

"Eighty thousand pounds!" Broadmoor exclaimed. "He is a bigger fool than I feared."

"I wish you would not speak so harshly of your cousin."

"Madam, I shall have far harsher words when I see him!"

"It is the work of that *harlot*." Anne shook her fan as if to fend off an imaginary foe. "A sorceress, that one. The blood of pagans runs in her veins. Her kind practice the black arts. Yes, that is how she swindled my Edward. She ought to be run out of England!"

He narrowed his eyes. "Of whom do you speak?"

"*Darcy Sherwood*." Anne shuddered. "Her sister and stepmother are the most common of common, but Miss Sherwood is the worst of them all! I hear the Sherwoods are in no small way of debt. No doubt they are only too happy to put their greedy hands upon our precious estate! I wonder that the darkie, that wench, had orchestrated the entire episode to avenge herself for what Edward had done to her sister—as if a gentleman of his stature could possibly look upon such a common young woman with *any* interest."

It had been five years, but Broadmoor remembered the Sherwood name. Only it had been Priscilla Sherwood that had posed the problem then. He had not thought the young lady a suitable match for Edward, who had formed an unexpected attachment to her, and severed the relationship between the two lovebirds by removing his cousin to Paris, where Edward had promptly forgotten about Priscilla in favor of the pretty French girls with their charming accents.

But Broadmoor had only vague recollections of Miss Darcy Sherwood, the elder of the Sherwood sisters.

"Oh, wretched, wretched is our lot!" Anne continued. "To think that we could be turned out of our own home by that piece of jade."

"That will not happen," Broadmoor pronounced, setting down his glass. Perhaps Anne was right and he should have taken more of an interest in Edward's affairs.

Relief washed over Anne. "How grand you are, Radcliff! If anyone can save our family, it is you! Your father and mother, bless their souls, would have been proud of you."

His thoughts turned to the woman upstairs. Penelope would not be pleased, but he meant to have his horse saddled immediately. His first visit would be to Mr. Thornsdale, a trusted friend of the family, to confirm the facts of what Anne had relayed to him.

And if Anne had the truth, his second visit would be to Miss Darcy Sherwood.

*That wicked harlot.*

# CHAPTER TWO

No one noticed the gentleman sitting in the dark corner of Mrs. Tillinghast's modest card-room. If they had, they would have immediately discerned him to be a man of distinction, possibly a member of the *ton*. His attire was simple but elegant, his cravat sharply tied, his black leather boots polished to perfection. On his right hand, he wore a signet bearing the seal of his title, the Baron Broadmoor.

Upon closer inspection, they would have found the edition of *The Times* that he held before him and pretended to read was over two days old. Why he should be reading the paper instead of participating in the revelry at the card tables was a mystery unto itself. No one came to Mrs. Tillinghast's gaming house to *read*. They came for three distinct reasons: the friendly tables, the surprisingly good burgundy, and a young woman named Miss Darcy Sherwood.

*That wicked harlot.*

Somewhere in the room a clock chimed the midnight hour, but the wine had been flowing freely for hours, making her partakers deaf to anything but the merriment immediately surrounding them. From the free manner in which the men and women interacted—one woman seemed to have her arse permanently affixed to the lap of her beaux while another boasted a décolletage so low her nipples peered above its lace trim—the Baron wondered that the gaming house might not be better deemed a brothel.

The only person to eventually take notice of Radcliff Barrington was a flaxen-haired beauty, but after providing a curt answer to her greeting without even setting down his paper, he was rewarded with an indignant snort and a return to his solitude. He rubbed his temple as he recalled how he had left the hysterics of his aunt only to be met upstairs with a tirade from his mistress about the impolitesse and hauteur of Anne Barrington to come calling at the residence of a woman she had hitherto acknowledged with the barest of civilities. After noting that the waistcoat upon the chair had disappeared upon his return, Broadmoor had turned the full weight of his stare upon Penelope, who instantly cowered and, upon hearing that he was to take his leave, professed that naturally he must attend to the affairs of his family with due speed.

A lyrical laughter transcending the steady murmur of conversation and merrymaking broke into his reverie. It was followed by a cacophony of men exclaiming "Miss Sherwood! Miss Sherwood!" and begging of said personage to grace their gaming table of faro or piquet. Peering over his paper, Broadmoor paused. For a moment, he could not reconcile the woman he beheld to the devil incarnate his aunt had described.

Miss Darcy Sherwood had a distinct loveliness born of her mixed heritage. The gown of fashion, with its empire waist and diaphanous skirt, accentuated her curves. The pale yellow dress, which Broadmoor noted was wearing thin with wear, would have looked unexceptional on most Englishwomen, but against her caramel toned skin, it radiated like sunshine.

Her hair lacked shine or vibrancy in color, but the abundance of tight full curls framed her countenance with both softness and an alluring unruliness. However, it was her bright brown eyes, fringed with long curved lashes, and her luminous smile that struck Broadmoor the most. It was unlike the demure turn at the corners of the lips that he was accustomed to seeing.

He felt an odd desire to whisk her away from the cads and hounds that descended upon her like vultures about a kill. But this protective instinct was shortlived when he saw her choice of companions was one James Newcastle.

Miss Sherwood could not have been much more than twenty-five years of age. Newcastle was nearly twice that, and it was all but common knowledge that he buggered his female servants, most of whom were former slaves before the British court finally banned the practice from the Isles. But then, the man was worth a hefty sum, having benefitted tremendously from his business in the American slave trade.

"A song, Miss Sherwood!" cried Mr. Rutgers. "I offer twenty quid for the chance to win a song."

"Offer fifty and I shall make it a *private performance*," responded Miss Sherwood gaily as she settled at the card table.

She was no better than a common trollop, Broadmoor decided, trading her favors for money. He felt his blood race to think that the fate of his family rested in the hands of such a hussy. He could tell from the swiftness with which she shuffled, cut, and then dealt the cards that she spent many hours at the tables. Her hands plied the cards like those of an expert pianist over the ivories. He was surprised that her hands could retain such deftness after watching her consume two glasses of wine within the hour and welcome a third. He shook his head.

*Shameless.*

Broadmoor felt as if he had seen enough of her unrefined behavior, but something about her compelled him to stay. Miss Sherwood, who had begun slurring her words and laughing at unwarranted moments as the night wore on, seemed to enjoy the attentions, but despite her obvious inebriation, her laughter sounded forced. There were instances when he thought he saw sadness in her eyes, but they were fleeting, like illusions taunting the fevered brain.

It was foolhardy for a woman to let down her guard in such company. She would require more than the assistance of the aging butler and scrawny page he had noticed earlier to keep these hounds at bay. Could it possibly be a sense of chivalry that obliged him to stay even as he believed that a woman of her sort deserved the fate that she was recklessly enticing? His family and friends would have been astounded to think it possible.

"My word, but Lady Luck has favored you tonight!" Rutgers exclaimed to Miss Sherwood, who had won her fourth hand in a row.

"Miss Sherwood has been in Her Company the whole week," remarked Mr. Wempole, a local banker, "since winning the deed to Brayten. I daresay you may soon pay off your debts to me."

Broadmoor ground his teeth at the mention of his late uncle's estate and barely noticed the flush that had crept up Miss Sherwood's face.

"It was quite unexpected," Miss Sherwood responded. "I rather think that I might—"

"That were no luck but pure skill!" declared Viscount Wyndham, the future Earl of Brent.

"Alas, I have lost my final pound tonight and have no hope of winning a song from Miss Sherwood," lamented Rutgers.

"I would play one final round," said Miss Sherwood as she shuffled the deck, the cards falling from her slender fingers with a contented sigh, "but brag is best played with at least a fourth."

"Permit me," said Broadmoor, emerging from the shadows. He reasoned to himself that he very much desired to put the chit in her place, but that could only partly explain why he was drawn to her table.

She raised an eyebrow before appraising him with a gaze that swept from the top of his head to the bottom of his gleaming boots. "We welcome all manner of strangers—especially those with ample purses."

*Brazen jade,* Broadmoor thought to himself as he took a seat opposite her and pulled out his money.

"S'blood," the schoolboy groused immediately after the cards were dealt and reached for a bottle of burgundy to refill his glass.

Glancing up from the three cards he held, Broadmoor found Miss Sherwood staring at him with an intensity that pinned him to his chair. The corners of her mouth turned upward as her head tilted ever so slightly to the side. Looking at her sensuously full lips, Broadmoor could easily see how she had all the men here in the palm of her hand. He wondered, briefly, how those lips would feel under his.

"Our cards are known to be friendly to newcomers," she informed him. "I hope they do not fail to disappoint."

He gave only a small smile. She thought him a naïve novice if she expected him to reveal anything of the hand that he held.

Darcy turned her watchful eye to Newcastle, whose brow was furrowed in deep concentration. She leaned towards him—her breasts nearly grazing the top of the table—and playfully tapped him on the forearm. "Lady Luck can pass you by no longer for surely your patience will warrant her good graces."

Radcliff tried not to notice the two lush orbs pushed and separated above her bodice. He shifted uncomfortably in his seat for despite his inclination to find himself at odds with anything Anne said, he was beginning to believe his aunt. Miss Sherwood possessed a beauty and aura that was like the call of Sirens, luring men to their doom. His own cock stirred with a mind of its own.

His slight movement seemed to catch her eye instantly, but she responded only by reaching for her glass of wine. After taking a long drink, she slammed the glass down upon the table. "Shall we make our last round for the evening the most dramatic, my dears? I shall offer a song—and a kiss…"

A murmur of excitement mixed with hooting and hollering waved over the room.

"…worth a hundred quid," she finished.

"S'blood," the schoolboy grumbled again after opening his purse to find he did not have the requisite amount. He threw his cards onto the table with disgust and grabbed the burgundy for consolation.

Newcastle pulled at his cravat, looked at his cards several times, before finally shaking his head sadly. Miss Sherwood fixed her gaze upon Radcliff next. He returned her stare and fancied that she actually seemed unsettled for the briefest of moments.

Almond brown. Her eyes were almond brown. And despite their piercing gaze, they seemed to be filled with warmth—like the comforting flame of a hearth in winter. Broadmoor decided it must be the wine that leant such an effect to her eyes. How like the Ironies in Life that she should possess such loveliness to cover a black soul.

"Shall we put an end to the game?" Miss Sherwood asked.

"As you please," Broadmoor replied without emotion. Her Siren's call would not work on him. "I will see your cards."

He pulled out two additional hundreds, placing the money on the table with a solemn deliberation that belied his eagerness.

Smiling triumphantly, Miss Sherwood displayed an ace of hearts, a king of diamonds, and a queen of diamonds.

"Though I would have welcomed a win, the joy was in the game," Newcastle said. "I could not derive more pleasure than in losing to you, Miss Sherwood."

Miss Sherwood smiled. "Nor could I ask for a more gallant opponent."

She reached for the money in the middle of the table, but Broadmoor caught her hand.

"It is as you say, Miss Sherwood," he said and revealed a running flush of spades. "Your cards are indeed friendly to newcomers."

For the first time that evening, Broadmoor saw her frown, but she recovered quickly. "Then I presume you will hence no longer be a stranger to our tables?"

Broadmoor was quiet as he collected the money.

"Beginner's luck," the schoolboy muttered.

Newcastle turned his attention to Broadmoor for the first time. "Good sir, I congratulate you on a most remarkable win. I am James Newcastle of Newcastle and Holmes Trading. Our offices are in Liverpool, but you may have heard of the company nonetheless. I should very much like to increase your winnings for the evening by offering you fifty pounds in exchange for Miss Sherwood's song and, er, kiss."

"I believe the song went for fifty and the kiss a hundred," Broadmoor responded.

"Er—yes. A hundred. That would make it a, er, hundred and fifty."

"I am quite content with what I have won. Indeed, I should like to delay no longer my claim to the first of my winnings."

"Very well," said Miss Sherwood cheerfully as she rose. "I but hope you will not regret that you declined the generous offer by Mr. Newcastle."

She headed towards the pianoforte in the corner of the room, but Broadmoor stopped her with his words.

"In *private*, Miss Sherwood."

In contrast to her confident manners all evening, Miss Sherwood seemed to hesitate before flashing him one of her most brilliant smiles. "Of course. But would you not care for a supper first? Or a glass of port in our dining room?"

"No."

"Very well. Then I shall escort you to our humble drawing room."

Broadmoor rose from his chair to follow her. From the corner of his eye, he saw Newcastle looking after them with both longing and consternation. As he passed out of the gaming room, he heard Rutgers mutter, "Lucky bloody bastard."

For a moment Broadmoor felt pleased with having won the game and the image of his mouth claiming hers flashed in his mind. What would her body feel like pressed to his? Those hips and breasts of hers were made to be grabbed...

But hers was a well traversed territory, he reminded himself. Based on his inquiries into Miss Sherwood, the woman changed lovers as frequently as if they were French fashion, and her skills at the card table were matched only by her skills in the bedchamber. The men spoke in almost wistful, tortured tones regarding the latter and often with an odd flush in the cheeks that Broadmoor found strange—and curious.

As with the card-room, the drawing room was modestly furnished. Various pieces were covered with black lacquer to disguise the ordinary quality of their components. A couple giggling in the corner took their leave upon the entry of Miss Sherwood, who closed the door behind him. Sitting down on a sofa that looked as if it might have been an expensive piece at one time but that age had rendered ragged in appearance, he crossed one long leg over another and watched as she went to sit down at the spinet.

Good God, even the way she walked made him warm in the loins. The movement accentuated the flare of her hips and the curve of her rump, neither of which her gown could hide. And yet she possessed a grace on par with the most seasoned ladies at Almack's. She did not walk as much as *glide* towards the spinet.

"Do you care for Mozart?" she asked.

"As you wish," he replied.

She chose an aria from *Le Nozze di Figaro*. The opera buffa with its subject of infidelity and its satirical underpinnings regarding the aristocracy seemed a fitting choice for her. Save for her middling pronunciation of Italian, Miss Sherwood might have done well as an opera singer. She sang with force, unrestrained. The room seemed too small to hold the voice wafting above the chords of the spinet. And she sang with surprising clarity, her fingers striking the keys with precision, undisturbed by the wine he had seen her consume. Despite her earlier displays of inebriation, she now held herself well, and he could not help but wonder if the intoxication had not all been an act.

"My compliments," he said when she had finished. "Though one could have had the entire opera performed for much less than fifty pounds, I can understand why one would easily wager such an amount for this privilege."

"Thank you, but you did so without ever having

heard me sing," she pointed out.

She wanted to know why, but he said simply, "I knew I would win."

Her brows rose at the challenge in his tone. The work of the devil could not always prevail. He ought bestir himself now to broach the matter that had compelled him here, but he found himself wanting to collect on the second part of his winnings: the kiss.

She rose from her bench, and his pulse pounded a faster beat. She smiled with the satisfaction of a cat that had sprung its trap on a mouse. "Would you care to test your confidence at our tables some more?"

"Are the bets here always this intriguing?" he returned.

"If you wish," she purred as she stood behind a small decorative table, a safe distance from him.

She began rearranging the flowers in a vase atop the table. "How is it you have not been here before?"

The teasing jade. If she did not kiss him soon, he would have to extract it for himself.

"I did not know its existence until today."

She studied him from above the flowers with a candor and length that no proper young woman would dare, but he did not mind her attempts to appraise him.

"You are new to London?"

Feeling restless, he stood up. He did not understand her hesitation. In the card room she had flaunted herself unabashed to any number of men, but now she chose to play coy with him?

"My preference is for Brooks's," he stated simply. "Tell me, Miss Sherwood, do your kisses always command a hundred pounds?"

Her lower lip dropped. His loins throbbed, and he

found he could not tear his gaze from the maddening allure of her mouth.

"Do the stakes frighten you?" she returned.

"I find it difficult to fathom any kiss to be worth that price."

"Then why did you ante?"

"As I've said, I knew I would win."

He could tell she was disconcerted, and when he took a step towards her, she glanced around herself as if in search of an escape.

Finding little room to maneuver, she lifted her chin and smiled. "Then care to double the wager?"

"Frankly, Miss Sherwood, for a hundred pounds, you ought to be offering far more than a kiss."

*As I am sure you have done*, he added silently. He was standing at the table and could easily have reached across it for her.

Her eyes narrowed at him. No doubt she was more accustomed to men who became simpering puppies at her feet. Perhaps she was affronted by his tone. But he little cared. She was too close to him, her aura more inviting than the scent of the flowers that separated them. He was about to avail himself of his prize when a knock sounded at the door.

"Yes?" Miss Sherwood called with too much relief.

The page popped his head into the room. "Mistress Tillinghast requested a word with you, Miss Sherwood."

Miss Sherwood excused herself and walked past him. The room became dreary without her presence. Though at first he felt greatly agitated by the intrusion of the page, he now felt relieved. He had a purpose in coming here. And instead he was falling under her spell. Shaking off the warmth that she had engendered in his body, he forced his mind to the task at hand. Now that he had gathered his wits about him, he shook his head at himself. Was it because he had not completed bedding his mistress that he found himself so easily captivated by Miss Sherwood?

He could see how this place could retain so many patrons and ensnare those of lesser fortitude and prudence like Edward. Even Mr. Thornsdale, whom Broadmoor would have thought more at home at White's than a common gaming hall such as this, revealed that he had known of Edward's increasing losses to Miss Sherwood because he himself was an occasional patron. Mr. Thornsdale had also offered, unsolicited, that he thought Miss Sherwood to be rather charming.

But Broadmoor doubted that he would find her as charming. The fourth Baron Broadmoor had a single objective in seeking out Miss Darcy Sherwood: to wrest from the wicked harlot what rightfully belonged to his family. And he meant to do so at any cost.

# CHAPTER THREE

"Now who do you suppose that tasty morsel of a stranger be?" wondered Mathilda Tillinghast—dubbed 'Mrs. T' by her gaming hall patrons—as she observed Darcy staring into the vanity mirror. Once a beauty who could summon a dozen men to her feet with a simple drop of her nosegay, Mathilda was now content to use Darcy as the main attraction of the gaming hall. "I find the air of mystery about him quite alluring."

"I thought for certain that I had correctly appraised his position," Darcy said, still wondering how she had lost that hand of brag. She had begun working at the gaming hall ever since her father, Jonathan Sherwood, had passed away ten years ago and left the family the remains of a sizeable debt, and rarely misjudged an opponent. What was it about the stranger that had sent her thoughts scattering like those of a schoolgirl?

She was both intrigued and unsettled by him. Instead of luring him into more rounds at the card tables—and the kiss would have been a perfect bait with any other man—she found herself *timid*.

Mathilda would have found it incomprehensible that she, Darcy Sherwood, who had taken many a man to her bed in more ways than most women could imagine, should be afraid of a simple kiss. When the page had appeared, she could not wait to escape and was now reluctant to leave the refuge of Mathilda's boudoir.

"How could I have lost?" she wondered aloud.

Mathilda snorted. "You sound as if you were in mourning, m'dear. Tisn't as if you lost any money. Wouldn't mind taking your place, in fact. Would that I were your age again. Give you a run for your money I would, 'cept for Newcastle maybe—you can have him."

Darcy shuddered. "If he had not boasted of how well his former slaves were treated—'better than courtesans,' were his words—and then to say that these women ought to be grateful for his kindness—I might have developed a conscience towards him. But knowing that his wealth comes from that horrible trade that ought to be outlawed if only Parliament would listen to Sir Wilberforce, I have no remorse of relieving him of some of that money."

"He can easily afford it, m'dear. They all deserve what they get if they are fool enough to fall for a pretty face."

"Who deserves it?" blurted Henry Perceville, Viscount Wyndham, as he entered the room unannounced and threw himself on the rickety bed. Despite his slender build, the mattress promptly sank beneath his weight. His golden locks fell across a pair of eyes that sparkled with merriment.

"Men," Mathilda answered.

"Nonetheless," said Darcy as she tucked an unruly curl behind her ear, "I should be relieved to give up the charade and restore what little dignity is left for me. Never to have to counterfeit another interested smile or to feign enjoyment at being fondled by every Dick and Harry…to be free…"

"You have the means to end the charade this instant—you have the deed to Brayten!" protested Henry.

"Which I mean to return. I feel as if I have fleeced a babe."

Henry rolled his eyes. "What a ninny you are. Edward Barrington is no innocent, as evidenced by what he did to your sister."

Darcy pressed her lips into a firm line. It had been five years, but the wound flared as strong as ever. She adored her sister Priscilla, her junior by four years, and whom she had always sought to protect. Edward had not only wronged Priscilla, but in so doing, had wronged Nathan, an innocent boy born without a father.

"How you can have the slightest sympathy for that pup confounds me," agreed Mathilda.

"I will never forgive the Barringtons for their mistreatment of Priscilla," Darcy acknowledged. "But I could not send a man and his family to ruin in such a fashion."

"That folly were his own creation. It was not your idea to offer up his own estate for a wager."

"If I offer to return Brayten in exchange for what Edward had initially lost to me, I could pay off our debts to Mr. Wempole and have enough to live comfortably for many years. Eighty thousand pounds were no paltry sum."

Henry threw his legs off the bed and sat up to face Darcy. "I am your oldest and dearest friend, and I must say that if you dare return Brayten to that Barrington fellow, I will never speak to you again. At the very least, wait a sennight before making your mind."

"Make the rascal squirm a might," agreed Mathilda. "I had meant to tell you that Mr. Reynolds has returned, and I think he is willing to open his purse a great deal more tonight—with the appropriate persuasion, of course. But this delectable stranger is far more promising."

Darcy blushed, turning away but not before Henry noticed.

"Do my eyes deceive?" he inquired. "Are you interested in this fellow?"

"He is different," Darcy admitted, recalling the most intense pair of eyes she had ever seen.

"Simply because a man refrains from ogling you or pawing you does not make him different from the others, darling. Oldest trick in the book."

"Am I not old enough to know all manner of tricks?" Darcy replied. "It amuses me how often men overestimate the appeal of their sex."

"They serve their purpose," added Mathilda with an almost sentimental wistfulness before taking a practical tone, "but like a banquet, one must sample a variety. Our Darcy will not be turned by one man alone, no matter how appetizing he appears."

"The only use I have of men, save you, dear Harry, is their pocketbooks," said Darcy firmly before taking her leave.

Despite her parting words, however, before returning to the drawing room where *he* waited, Darcy stopped at a mirror in the hallway to consider her appearance. She found herself concerned with how the stranger might perceive her. An entirely silly feeling more appropriate to a chit out of the schoolroom than an experienced woman such as herself. She wasn't even sure that the man liked her. Indeed, she rather suspicioned that he did not, despite his having wagered for her kiss. Nonetheless, she confirmed that the sleeves of her gown were even and that her hair was tucked more or less in place.

"Never thought to find you here, Lord Broadmoor."

It was the voice of Cavin Richards, a notorious rake known among women for his seductive grin and among men for his many female conquests.

Broadmoor, Darcy repeated to herself. The name was vaguely familiar.

"And your presence here surprises me none at all," was the uninterested response from the stranger in the drawing room.

Not put off, Cavin replied, "Yes, I find White's and Brooks's rather dull in comparison to Mrs. T's. Care for a round of hazard?"

"I came not for cards or dice but to see Miss Sherwood."

"Ahhhh, of course, *Miss Sherwood.*"

Darcy was familiar with the suggestive smile that Cavin was no doubt casting at the stranger. She held herself against the wall but inched closer towards the open doors.

"Quite pleasurable to the eye, is she not?" Cavin drawled.

"She is tolerable."

"Tolerable? My friend, you are either blind in an eye or have odd standards of beauty."

"While I find her appearance does no offense, it cannot hide the vulgarity of her nature."

Darcy bit her bottom lip. She supposed she had played the flirt quite heavily tonight, but had she been that offensive?

"Vulgarity of nature?" Cavin echoed. "I agree Miss Sherwood is no candidate for Almack's but that's playing it up strong. Or is it her vulgarity what draws you? I must say, I never saw that side of you, Broadmoor. I own that I thought you rather a bore, but now you intrigue me!"

The irritation in his voice was evident as Broadmoor responded, "It is clear to me that you know little of me, Richards, and perhaps less of Miss Sherwood or even you would not be so ready to consort in her company. I know your standards to be *pliant,* but I did not think they would extend to the lowest forms of humankind. Indeed, I would barely put Miss Sherwood above the snail or any other creature that crawls with its belly to the earth. For beauty or not, I would rather be seen with a carnival animal than in her company. It is with the greatest displeasure that circumstances have compelled—nay, forced—me to call upon her. I would that I had nothing to do with her, her family, or any of her ilk."

"Then what extraordinary occasion would bring my lordship from his Olympus to consort with us lower mortals?" Darcy asked upon her appearance in the drawing room, relieved that her voice did not quiver quite as much as she had feared it would for it was difficult to contain the anger that flared within her.

The Baron seemed taken aback but quickly collected himself. His bow to her was exceedingly low, but the ice in his tone would have sent shivers down the most stalwart man. "Miss Sherwood, I have matters to dispense that I trust will not require much of your time or mine."

He turned to Cavin and added, "In private."

Darcy could tell from his eager expression that her former lover desired very much to stay, but she had no interest in his presence either.

"My invitation to hazard remains open should you decide to stay," Cavin told Broadmoor as he picked up his hat and gloves, winking at Darcy before departing.

With Cavin gone, Darcy placed the full weight of her gaze upon the Baron. She lifted her chin as if that alone gave her height enough to match his.

"I think you know why I have come to call," Broadmoor said without a wasted second.

"It was not for my song?" She hoped her flippant tone covered how much his earlier words had stung her.

"Do not play your games with me, my child."

Games? What was he getting at?

"Then what game do you wish to play, sir, brag apparently not being sufficient for you?"

Her response seemed to ignite flames in his eyes. He took a menacing step towards her, his lips pressed into a thin line. "It would be unwise of you to incur my wrath."

"And you mine," she responded before thinking. She was not about to allow him browbeat her.

He looked surprised, then amused to the point of

laughter. She took that moment to move towards the sideboard for despite her desire to challenge him word for word and gaze for gaze, his nearness was beginning to intimidate her.

"I am prepared to offer a great sum for the return of the deed to Brayten," he announced. "I am told that the circumstances of the wager between you and my cousin were fair. For that reason alone, I offer recompense."

It was then that Darcy recognized the eyes—the same color of coal as Edward Barrington, who sported much lighter hair and whose lanky form did not match his cousin's imposing physique. Her mind sank into the recesses of her mind to connect the name of Broadmoor with one Radcliff Barrington.

She had heard only that his manner tended towards the aloof. She should not be surprised that, like his cousin, he tended towards the arrogant as well, but nothing had quite prepared her for the condescension that overflowed with each deliberate word of his.

"Pray, what great sum are you offering?" she asked with nonchalance as she poured herself a glass of burgundy.

"The proposal of a monetary recompense interests you, I see," he noted.

How she wished she could turn the lout into stone with her glare. Instead, she feigned a sweet smile and said, "Yes, we lower creatures of the earth prefer the petty and base interests."

"I am prepared to offer one hundred thousand pounds, Miss Sherwood."

Darcy began choking on the wine she had tried to imbibe just then. After coughing and sputtering and feeling as if her face must have matched her beverage in color, she straightened herself.

One hundred thousand pounds...it was enough to discharge the debts and provide a decent living for her family. By returning Brayten, her intention from the start, she could have done with the gaming house. She was tempted to take his offer without a second thought, but various words he had said rang in her head. Had he called her a child earlier?

"Your cousin was in debt to me for eighty thousand pounds before he lost Brayten," she said, stalling. "One could say you are offering me only twenty thousand pounds for Brayten. I think the estate to be worth far more than that, surely?"

His eyes were flint, and her heart beat faster as she tried to ignore the way his stare bored into her.

"What sum would you find more appropriate?"

The question stumped Darcy. She had no impression of what Brayten could actually be worth.

"Two hundred thousand pounds?" she guessed.

This time it was Broadmoor's turn to choke and turn color. "You are refreshingly forthright of your greed. I have known many indulgent people in the course of my life, but you, Miss Sherwood, are the epitome of cupidity!"

"And you, sir, are the epitome of insolence!" she returned.

As if sensing that the gloves had come off, Broadmoor sneered, "I am relieved to discard our pretenses of civility. My courtesy is wasted on a wanton jade."

"If you think your impertinence will aid your efforts to reclaim Brayten at a lower sum, you are a poor negotiator!"

"My offer stems from my generosity. I could easily consult my barristers and find another means of retrieving what is mine."

"Then speak to your barristers and do not misuse my time!"

The words flew from her mouth before she had a chance to consider them. She wondered for a moment if she were being unwise but then decided she didn't care.

In his displeasure, he clenched his jaw, causing a muscle in his face to ripple. "You may find my cousin easy prey, but I assure you that I am no fool."

"How comforting," Darcy could not resist.

"Impudent trollop! I have a mind to drag you into the street for a public whipping!"

Unable to fend off her anger, Darcy glared at him and declared, "You have persuaded me that to part with Brayten for anything less than three hundred thousand pounds would be folly."

"Jezebel! Are there no limits to your wickedness?"

Darcy shrugged and looked away. Her heart was pounding madly.

"I see plainly what is afoot," Broadmoor observed. "You mean to punish me for taking Edward from your sister."

She glanced sharply at him. "You! You took Edward?"

"A most wise decision on my part, for I would rather see him in hell than attached to a family such as yours!"

Her heart grew heavy as she remembered Priscilla's pain and thought of the life that should have been afforded to Nathan had Edward done right by them both.

And it was apparently the doing of Edward's arrogant cousin!

"I would not return Brayten to you for the world!" Darcy cried. "If I were a man, I should throw you from the house. You are a lout and a mucker!"

He took a furious step towards her. "You ought consider yourself fortunate, Miss Sherwood, not to be a man else I would not hesitate to box your ears in. You do not deserve the decency afforded to a trull..."

A trull was she? A Jezebel. A jade. She had heard worse, but coming from him, the words were fuel to a fire already burning out of control. What else was it that he had said? *For beauty or not, I would rather be seen with a carnival animal than in her company...*

"I will consider your exchange under one condition," she said. "You will submit to being my suitor—*an ardent suitor*—for a period of six months. You will tend to my every wish and command. Only then, upon your satisfactory and unconditional submission, will I relinquish the deed to Brayten."

He stared at her in disbelief before smirking. "You suffer delusions of grandeur. I am not in the habit of courting sluts."

"Then I suggest you begin practicing," she replied, feeling triumphant to see the veins in his neck pulsing rapidly. "You will appear no later than ten o'clock each evening and await my directions. You will speak not a word of this arrangement to anyone or I am sure to find Brayten beautiful this time of year."

Broadmoor was beyond livid. He grabbed her with both of his hands. "Damnable doxy! I shall see you thrown in gaol for your treachery and have no remorse if you perished there."

He was holding her so close that she could feel his angry breath upon her cheek. She tried to ignore the rapid beating of her heart and the painful manner in which her arms were locked in his vice. He looked as if he desired to snap her in twain—and could no doubt accomplish it rather easily in his current state of wrath. It took all her courage to force out words.

"Unhand me, Baron—lest you wish to pay for the privilege of your touch."

At first he drew her closer. Darcy held her breath. But then he threw her from him in disgust as if she possessed a contagion. Grabbing his gloves and cane, he strode out of the room. Darcy watched his anger with pleasure, but a small voice inside warned her that she had just awoken a sleeping tiger.

# OTHER WORKS BY
# GEORGETTE BROWN